Dedalus Original Fiction in Paperback

The Secret Knowledge

Andrew Crumey was born in Glasgow in 1961. He read theoretical physics and mathematics at St Andrews University and Imperial College in London, before doing post-doctoral research at Leeds University on nonlinear dynamics.

After a spell as the literary editor at *Scotland on Sunday* he now combines teaching creative writing at Northumbria University with his writing. He lives in Newcastle-upon-Tyne.

His first novel *Music, in a Foreign Language* (1994) was awarded The Saltire Best First Book Prize. His second novel *Pfitz* (1995) was one of the books of the year for *The Observer* and *The New York Times*. *D'Alembert's Principle* was published to great acclaim in 1996. *Mr Mee* (2000), *Mobius Dick* (2004) and *Sputnik Caledonia* (2008) followed. His novels have been translated into 13 languages.

Andrew Crumey

The Secret
Knowledge

Dedalus

Supported using public funding by
**ARTS COUNCIL
ENGLAND**

Published in the UK by Dedalus Limited,
24-26, St Judith's Lane, Sawtry, Cambs, PE28 5XE
email: info@dedalusbooks.com
www.dedalusbooks.com

ISBN printed book 978 1 909232 45 7
ISBN ebook 978 1 909232 56 3

Dedalus is distributed in the USA by SCB Distributors,
15608 South New Century Drive, Gardena, CA 90248
email: info@scbdistributors.com   web: www.scbdistributors.com

Dedalus is distributed in Australia by Peribo Pty Ltd.
58, Beaumont Road, Mount Kuring-gai, N.S.W. 2080
email: info@peribo.com.au

First published by Dedalus in 2013
The Secret Knowledge copyright © Andrew Crumey 2013

Printed in Finland by Bookwell
Typeset by Marie Lane

A C.I.P. listing for this book is available on request.

Acknowledgements

This work was partly supported by a grant from the Arts and Humanities Research Council, for research carried out at Newcastle University. Further work was done at St John's College, Durham, while the author was visiting fellow at Durham Institute of Advanced Study.

1913

Paris

Yvette has been told that the big wheel is incredible, but now that she stands before it in the park there is something comfortingly domestic about its appearance. The great metal-spoked circle is like an oversized bicycle wheel, slowly whirring its passengers upwards into amazement as they stand in the blue-painted wooden carriages dangling merrily from the revolving rim. From where she watches, Yvette is unable to make out individual faces through the glass panes of those distant compartments; instead she sees the eagerness of insects.

With the warm July sunshine on her neck, Yvette waits, pricking the shadowed gravel at her feet with the point of her folded parasol. Pierre ought to be here by now; he said noon, but the clock on the tower shows ten minutes past twelve, and among the throng of people in the park, his face remains invisible to her. What could have detained him? He has never been as late as this, his delay only confirming the ominousness she detected already in the note he sent, cryptically referring to a "matter of great significance". It seemed an implicit proposal of marriage, now it feels more like a warning of disaster. He's had second thoughts. He loves another.

Yvette is twenty-one and already many of her childhood friends are married. Some have children of their own. She looks once more at the big wheel, slowly depositing passengers and accepting new ones from the head of the queue that snakes far behind the pennanted ticket tent. She can make out an entire family – mother and father, three children of varying heights, a grandmother or aunt – all shuffling eagerly into the stationary compartment whose door lies open for them, while the preceding passengers leave from the far side. One day, Yvette thinks, she will be the mother. One day she will have been grandmother.

When Pierre speaks of love he mostly refers to music. He is studying at the conservatory; soon, he assures her, the name of Pierre Klauer will be known around the world. She adores hearing him speak that way, though to her untrained ear his music is unfathomable. He can play Beethoven piano sonatas with the smoothness of an expert yet in his own compositions he favours harsh rhythms, jangling discords. She has always thought of art as being a matter of beauty and refinement, but the new kind is about something else, progress and modernity, even if that means sacrificing old laws of taste. He says it is the sound of the future. She only hopes there will be room in it for her.

The wheel recommences operation, revolving at its full, stately speed. The family she saw are gliding over the top, the children shoving for a better view. Yvette can imagine the commotion inside the wooden compartment, the father's stern injunctions to order. Her own parents know about Pierre and naturally approve of him; his father has made a fortune from factories in Germany and Pierre need never work, though he has excellent prospects as an organist or teacher in one of the best schools. Any obstacle would more likely come from Pierre's side, since Yvette's father is only a furniture dealer who, for all that he has achieved, is in some people's eyes no better than a shopkeeper.

It is a long while for a woman to stand alone. Eyes have been noticing her; young men tip their hats, smile, stroke their moustaches in gestures of invitation or enquiry. So many men have passed her in these extended minutes, most with a partner or friend, but others alone, like herself, and it is only her very deliberate turning away from them – at one point even waving to an imaginary far-off Pierre – that has prevented some from speaking.

She decides to wait less conspicuously, near a row of whitewashed stalls where people are tossing hoops at upright bottles, aiming darts at targets, buying cups of lemonade. Yvette places herself at the end of the row, beside a glazed booth from which candied fruits are being sold. Sunlight shines through its yellow pane onto Yvette's dress, dappling it with light. A butterfly, impressed by the topaz glow, flits intently about her, as if trying to suck nectar from the coloured air. Afraid at first, Yvette calms her nervousness of the darting creature and watches while it briefly keeps her company before speeding away above the bobbing hats of the chatting crowd.

Pierre speaks of a revolution in art; the kind of talk they can share as lovers, but best kept from the misunderstanding ears of parents. She has spent three weeks without seeing him, the longest separation since their relationship began – and only four letters to console her. He has been staying with friends outside Paris, working on an important composition. She has no reason to doubt him.

Three young men, common labourers by the look of them, are taking turns to fling balls at a pyramid of cans, their sleeves rolled up, perspiration gleaming on their unshaved faces. Probably here after a long night-shift but still with ox-like strength, lusting for pleasure more than sleep. One of them gives her a glance before flexing his muscular arm and sending the tins flying. What would these fellows make of the new art? Brahms and Wagner failed to save humanity; how can Pierre? Yet that is his dream: to improve the world. Revolutionary music is not enough; there has to be a change in the whole of human affairs, a modulation into a new key. If she did not know him well enough she might fear he was a communist. She wonders about his new friends.

And then at last his voice. "Yvette! Thanks goodness!"

"Pierre!"

After so much waiting there is a sense of both joy and awkwardness, because although his white suit and straw hat, his black tie and the flower in his buttonhole are all familiar, she thinks he looks somehow different, as though a year has passed since they last saw each other. When he bends to kiss her hand she detects his father's Teutonic formality; there is something new in the smile he raises from her fingertips, as though he might like to bite her. His teeth are whiter than she remembers.

"I've missed you, Pierre."

"It's wonderful to see you. Let's walk."

Arm in arm they stroll across the park that had become for Yvette a blur of worry. "Are you truly glad?"

"Of course!"

"But I think your mind is somewhere else."

"It has been."

They pause at the entrance to a tent where Pierre is distracted by the sight of a wooden dummy standing as advertisement for whatever goes on inside: a dainty female figure with a brightly painted face, like a fairy or ballet dancer, and Yvette thinks to herself, after three weeks of longing it should not be like this. He cares more about a piece of wood than about me! "Do you want to go inside?"

"What? No, it reminded me of something, that's all."

She can take no more. "Do you love me?"

He splutters, not sure at first if she is joking, then sees the seriousness on her face. "How can you doubt it?

"Is there another you prefer?"

He embraces her. "You know you're everything to me."

"Then why keep me waiting and arrive with no apology? Why be so distant?"

He looks down at his feet like a humbled schoolboy. "I've been working hard, creating such marvellous music." When he raises his eyes she sees in their sparkle a vulnerability that melts her fear. "You know I'll always have two loves, Yvette."

"Yes, I know that." Her mind focuses on that comforting word: always.

"I've begun writing a symphony."

"How wonderful!" It means nothing to her except a sudden vision of being seated in a grand concert hall wearing an exquisite dress bought specially for the occasion, diamonds glittering on her skin. She sees herself bathed in the admiration of the elite.

"Of course it might never be heard," Pierre adds. "It's a private commission."

"From one of your new friends?"

"Never mind." He takes her hand and leads her away from

the tent with a sudden light-hearted swiftness in his step that makes her giddy with relief. "Let's laugh and enjoy ourselves, Yvette. Let's celebrate the future!"

"Yes!"

He wants to try throwing hoops and wins a ridiculous rosette that has them both giggling. They go to the little boating lake where there is a long queue that makes him impatient, perhaps they should have candy floss instead. "And what about the big wheel?" Yvette keeps asking. "When do we go on it?" He says they must save it for the right moment.

They walk along the tree-lined avenue, and Yvette playfully demands to know more about the new music, the new friends. "Are they artists?"

"A variety of people. Dreamers and scholars; an intellectual fraternity."

"I only hope you won't keep disappearing to be with them."

"I promise you, I won't. I want us to be together, Yvette."

"You said you were staying with them; where exactly?"

He speaks breezily. "Here and there…"

"Where?"

He can see she demands detail. "Mostly at a place near Compiègne. A quiet, peaceful house with a good piano, perfect for composing. The owner's a man of great power and influence."

"What's his name?"

"I can't tell you that, Yvette. He wants me to write the symphony, he's paying me for it, but he doesn't wish his involvement to be known."

"Not even to me, your… your… friend?"

"I'm sorry, Yvette, I hate to be so secretive. Eventually you'll understand the reason."

"Then can you at least tell me about your music?" All her

doubts are crowding back. the fine house with its wealthy owner, the colony of artists inhabiting it, even the piano and the music supposedly written on it, all seem like mirages meant to hide the single female fact that stands, a mighty odalisque, against her.

He tells her he has nearly finished composing the symphony on the keyboard but still needs to do the orchestration. "It's called *The Secret Knowledge*."

"A secret you can share with me?"

"Later."

"But why?" She stops and grips both his hands. "Pierre, I have qualms about this."

"Don't be foolish…"

"I know that you do, too, I can sense it. I thought you might have found another lover, but no, that's not what's wrong. You're afraid."

"Nonsense."

"I am too. I don't trust your mysterious patron or your intellectual friends. What does your father think?"

"It's better for him not to know."

She swings away wondering which possibility is more distressing: that he has been unfaithful, or that he could have fallen in with bad company. Yvette knows about the men who want revolution through violence rather than art. "You have to leave these friends of yours."

"Why?" He is behind her, putting his hands on her shoulders, she can feel herself flowing into his touch.

"Unless you can tell me exactly what's going on I can only fear the worst. I read the newspapers, Pierre, I know about the problems in the world. Only the other week there was that bomb that went off and killed so many people."

"It was in Serbia."

"How do I know your secret club isn't an anarchist clique?"

"I can assure you it isn't any such thing." He makes her turn and in his face she sees a childlike radiance. "I suppose you could say I'm a utopian, dreaming of an ideal world. Is there anything wrong in that?"

"Of course not."

"I want us to be together in that world. Forever." When he holds her close to his chest she thinks she feels rising inside him the great announcement he wants to make, his proposal of marriage. Not yet, though. Releasing her he says, "Let's go to the big wheel."

What he means is that she should stop asking questions, but while they walk to join the queue she finds it impossible. "You've always been lost in your ideas, Pierre, yet never so mysterious."

"It's only temporary, and for the best. When the time is right I'll tell you everything."

"And when will the time be right?"

"Soon."

They stand waiting in line with the families, couples, excited children and quietly curious grandparents. Pierre pays at the desk they reach and receives two blue tickets he holds aloft as though perusing their authenticity. "Let's keep these as souvenirs," he says.

"Of what?"

"Of this moment, right now, that will never come again for us."

She looks at them in his hand, small scraps of coloured paper, and the bad feeling is in her throat and chest, the nauseous sense of foreboding. At the head of the queue, people are being assisted into a waiting carriage, and to Yvette's eye there is something in all of it that resembles the herding of livestock. She watches the door being locked on a mother and father and their two children. Life is weightless, a falling through an endless void she can't quite picture or put a name to, but she senses it right now, in this moment that can never return.

She grips him suddenly. "Let's not."

"What?"

"I'm scared of it."

He laughs. "It's perfectly safe, Yvette, just look at everyone else."

"I don't care about everyone else, only us. Let's go back."

The bearded gentleman in front can be seen listening to the little crisis; his wife is speaking to him from under her broad hat but he isn't listening, instead his head is cocked to catch the drama played out behind.

"I paid for the tickets, Yvette." There is the faintest note of petulance in Pierre's voice.

"I'll pay you back."

"I didn't mean that. Are you honestly frightened of going up? I'll hold your hand, it'll be beautiful, I promise."

"It's not the ride I'm afraid of."

"Then what? Please let's do it, Yvette. It's how I planned it in my mind. How I've imagined it. You know there's something very important I want to say to you. Something that will affect us for the rest of our lives…"

She silences his lips with her fingertips. "All right. Enough, darling. Only promise me again, promise me with all your heart that it will be beautiful."

"I do."

Their turn arrives. The couple in front are shepherded into the empty wooden cabin that swings to a halt before them, then Pierre and Yvette are invited too, as well as two young men behind. It all happens so swiftly and easily, Yvette thinks, watching through the glass window while the attendant bars the door firmly shut. She grips Pierre to steady herself when with a sudden lurch the cabin moves in an upward arc, making the passengers laugh nervously. It stops again for the performance to be repeated below, and before long they have all become accustomed to this new form of transport, giving them a slowly widening view of the surrounding park with each stage of the ascent.

"Aren't you glad?" Pierre whispers, and she nods. Did he always imagine there would be four strangers riding with them?

"I'm not afraid any more."

The remaining compartments are eventually filled; the wheel begins to rotate at a smooth and graceful pace, bringing the enraptured riders past a summit that makes them gasp with awe.

"I feel almost like a bird!" says one.

"The people are no bigger than ants."

Standing apart from the babble of excitement, Pierre's observations are more considered, as though he has thought in advance of the wheel's effect and significance. "The modern world makes everything seem small," he tells Yvette softly, the two of them pressing against a pane to see the approaching ground, the passing sweep of attendants standing idle, the commencement of the next orbit. "Life seen from a speeding window."

"Don't you like it?"

"The categories of like and dislike are outmoded."

She has heard him talk this way often enough about music, but now she knows he is referring to something else. "I suppose I must be old-fashioned, Pierre, I still believe in like and dislike. That's why I wonder about your friends."

"They've helped me see the world in a completely different manner. Not through a window at all. They speak of new laws of science: relativity, quantum theory."

"What does this have to do with us?"

"They've made me realise that every moment is a decision, a test. You thought of turning back, but didn't."

"Because I trust you."

"If we hadn't got on, it would only have made the tiniest difference to the world, but differences add up, everything matters."

"Are you saying that if I walked away it would have been the end?" The absurdity of the idea is what permits her to express it; Pierre seems to take it seriously.

"I don't know," he says. "I don't know what would have happened."

This is the test, then; her future happiness depends on a fairground ride. "Don't play games with me."

"I'm not, it's life that plays with us – a game of chance."

"I thought you believed in destiny."

"I believe in hope."

The carriage passes its apex once again; Yvette wonders how many more rounds there will be before the finish. "I also have my hopes, Pierre. Tell me whatever you have to."

"Two things," he says. "Two very great things on which the whole of my world now hinges." He clasps her hands. "Yvette, I want you to be my wife."

He has timed it imperfectly: they are not far from the ground. But others in the carriage catch the flavour of Yvette's rapturous response, they hear her acceptance, see the way she kisses and holds him, so that when they all reach the top there is a general mood of celebration, of quiet congratulation.

There are smiles and sighs, and a polite turning away to allow the couple a restoration of their privacy.

"I'm so happy, Pierre." She wipes a tear from her eye.

"I was very nervous about asking."

"Is that all? Is that why you were so strange?"

"I suppose."

She laughs. "You're so adorable!" A catalogue of plans passes through her imagination: the church, the dress, the guests. An entire future constructing itself in an instant out of the simplest, humblest materials, like a palace of playing cards, and at its foundation the parents whose permission will be needed: his proud German father. It worries her. "You said there were two things."

"Not here, my love."

The wheel slows to a halt and beneath them a carriage is unlocked. The spell has ended; the atmosphere in the compartment changes to an impatience to be freed. Waiting in silence, Yvette feels anxiety return like an inexorable tide. It was such a short and blissful experience, soaring free of gravity. "Give me the tickets," she says when their door is opened and they step into the dull terrestrial air.

"You see why I said we should keep them?" Crumpled from his pocket, they have the solemn mortality of fallen feathers. "This is the happiest day of my life, Yvette."

"And mine." She is a sleepwalker in two worlds at once, reality and dream; his proposal should have turned one into the other but hasn't, instead it has emphasised their separation. She wants someone to shake her by the shoulders, wake her, show her that the marriage has happened, the children are born.

He leads her back to the row of stalls that was their rendezvous; he wants to buy her something, a sweet biscuit perhaps, or a posy of flowers. He speaks rapidly as if trying to placate a child while thinking of more important matters only an adult can understand; he sounds nervous and evasive.

"Tell me now," she demands. "If I'm to be your wife there can be no more secrets."

"You must wait here for me," he says urgently.

"What?"

"I have to leave you for a few moments."

"Why?"

"As soon as I come back I'll explain everything, I promise. I will tell you the secret knowledge."

He has the face of a stranger, an emerging look of barely suppressed panic.

"You're going to meet one of them, aren't you?"

"Don't try to guess, Yvette, you can't possibly imagine… Please don't make this harder for me. I love you so much."

"Then why not trust me?"

"First I have to trust myself. My own destiny. Yvette, I believe in the better world that's approaching, I really do, but it won't come unless we make it happen. There are risks…"

"I can't believe you're doing this to me, after asking me to marry you. Do you want me to reject you? Is this the test you had in mind?"

He nods vigorously. "That's right, it's a test. Your test, Yvette. All you have to do is wait here for me. Five minutes. Wait here, and when I come back our future can begin."

"You mean this is like making me go on the big wheel?"

"Exactly."

His sinister friends have put him up to this ridiculous stunt, she knows it. He will come back and confess, then she must persuade him to forget about them forever.

"One thing, Yvette." He reaches inside his jacket and brings out something small, hidden in his fingers. A ring? No, what he holds before her is a key. "The manuscript – it's in a drawer of my desk." He gives her the key and she stares at it in bewilderment, not hearing his words. She raises her eyes and sees him already hurrying away.

"Pierre!"

He doesn't look back. Pierre goes in the direction of the boating pond, disappearing among the trees, but Yvette has lost sight of him before then, her eyes filled with tears. She holds the key so tightly that it hurts. This is the future he has promised: lies and deception. It has to be another woman. Pierre is a partisan of the avant-garde and she is not naive. There are secrets she will need to learn.

This is worse than her earlier wait, the fairground looks monstrous and hostile, every smile a taunt. What if she were to walk away? Can she not put Pierre to the test, make him prove himself worthy of her love? Is she to be nothing more than the muse of a genius? She can see the tent with the painted wooden dummy outside that made him pause. *Ariel: The Extraordinary Flying Girl*. The unseen show within becomes a sudden source of fascination for her. She wants to witness the spectacle, enjoy it alone while she is still free. Yes, free, without a ring on her finger. Only a key. With her gaze fixed stonily on the flapping canvas tent she walks toward it, clutching his ridiculous gift and wondering if she should toss it away like an apple core – his desk, his unscored symphony, his destiny. Growing before her eyes is the wooden figure of a diminutive flat-chested girl, a fairy beckoning with a fixed expression, so that Yvette sees nothing else, hears nothing, feels herself drawn inside the sprite's realm, being swung like an acrobat on a giant rotating wheel of fortune, and only gradually she realises that encroaching on her consciousness is a noise, a din, anguished shouts and a general rushing. Startled, she turns and sees a convergence like water in a funnel, a flow of people following others to discover what is going on near the boating pond where the crowd is densest, and she goes too, feeling herself pushed and jostled but with her senses dulled like a diver's at great depth, catching eventually, from distraught onlookers making their way back in her direction, that there has been an accident, a gun went off, a man is feared dead, and somehow she knows immediately who it must be, though it will be so long before she can ever bring herself to believe it. Yes, she keeps telling herself, it's the happiest day of my life. The happiest day of my life.

Chapter One

The venue is a provincial town hall, the concert an item in the annual local arts festival. Why was David Conroy invited to perform? Probably because among the better known pianists the organisers tried first, none were available, or all were too expensive. He didn't think of it while playing, the music mattered more to him than thoughts of his declining career, but standing beside the instrument to acknowledge applause for the final piece in his recital, he senses the disappointment of people who would have preferred tunes they already knew, played by someone whose name they recognised.

He walks from the stage and the clapping continues; they've paid good money and expect an encore, though some have trains to catch or restaurant tables waiting; he can see figures leaving while he returns and sits to give the obligatory bonus feature, Liszt's *Églogue* providing an envoi as civilised and unambiguous as coffee and mints. Departing the platform once more he is congratulated in the wings by the young female assistant who has gauged the diminishing ovation and politely shows him back to his dressing room.

He's not yet fifty but feels too old for this. Sitting alone in front of the mirror's tired reflection he checks his phone, there's a text from Laura, she hopes the tour is still going well. Tour is too grand a word for the three engagements that have taken him out of his college routine for a week. The truth is that he no longer tours, or records; the prize-winning rising star of three decades ago turned into a disappointed teacher who does occasional performances like this, off-circuit, low fee, barely more dignified than a church-hall vanity concert. Laura's text is concise, impersonal, the sort of thing she could have sent to one of her journalist colleagues. Their last interaction before parting was an argument about the fridge.

A knock on the dressing-room door, it's the assistant, Tiff. Bubbly and petite, she has immaculately bobbed hair and the limitless enthusiasm of someone at the beginning of what she considers a career. When she introduced herself earlier in the day she said she would be "handling things", and he said it would be a pleasure being handled by her. They both laughed.

Tiff has brought a few autograph hunters; two elderly ladies are shown in, enveloped in floral perfume and dressed smartly for their evening out. One has a limp and uses a walking stick, the taller is mannish with a wispy moustache. Both thank Conroy lavishly for his wonderful performance while he signs their programmes. "I particularly enjoyed the Beethoven," says the limping one, with the confident benevolence of a parish organiser. "Though I wasn't so keen on the modern piece." She means a suite by Luigi Firelli composed more than half a century ago, Conroy has always liked to include some twentieth-century repertoire, especially if the composer is unknown. Schoenberg or Stockhausen will half box-office returns at a stroke; Firelli's name is as obscure and innocuous as Conroy's own.

"The Schumann was remarkably fast," the taller woman

announces, looking at her signed programme as though it were an application form. "He went mad, didn't he?"

"Depression," Conroy corrects.

"Obvious from the music that he must have been disturbed."

The other interrupts to relate that she studied piano in her younger days, and on one occasion met Alfred Brendel, who was a family friend, and played Schubert for him, receiving great encouragement in return. So this is what she really came for, to share this piece of history that she can already see passing over the horizon of her existence. She wants the world to know that Alfred Brendel heard her play, liked it, and right now Conroy is the world. "Well done," he says, an invitation to leave that both women accept.

At the open doorway Tiff stands with a pale, earnest-looking teenage boy, next in line, who comes and holds out a notebook open at a double-page, the left sheet bearing a bold illegible scrawl. He points to the empty right.

"Would you like a message, a dedication?" Conroy asks.

"Only a signature."

It feels like checking in at the hotel earlier; Conroy wonders if the kid will want his car registration too. Just for the hell of it he tries making conversation. "I hope you enjoyed the music." The boy says nothing, which Conroy takes as a no, so he tries a different line. "What are you studying at school?"

"I'm at university. Physics."

"Really?" The surprise is that he's old enough to vote, not that he should be studying a subject in which he need never talk to anyone. "Have you worked out what happened to Schrödinger's cat?" This is pretty much the only problem of physics Conroy can think of, unless he asks if the kid knows how to fix fridges. He hands the book back.

"Schrödinger's cat?" the boy says, almost scornfully, as if

it were some elementary exam question. "I reckon we're all inside the box." He glances at the signature, closes the book and walks away.

That, thinks Conroy, is one reason why he was never cut out for this line of work – having to be nice to pricks just because they bought a ticket for the show. It looks like he's already reached the limit of his fan base for the night but then Tiff reappears with a final visitor, a plump, balding man in his thirties, jacket and tie, polite handshake, the air of a scholar, and when he compliments Conroy on his rubato, the welcome voice of a genuine connoisseur. "I particularly enjoyed the Firelli," he adds unexpectedly. "In fact it was why I came, I have a special interest in twentieth-century music, rather a large collection."

"Of recordings?"

"Scores, first editions, some manuscripts."

This is an agreeable surprise. Both of them, it transpires, are interested in "minor" composers, though it is a term neither of them cares to use, their interest being premised on the denial of such facile pigeonholing. They trade a few names; Timman's *Rembrandt Sonata* is one the collector knows, in fact from Conroy's own recording of it made fifteen years ago, likewise Hessel's *Tapestry*, though DuFoy's *Prolegomena* is as unfamiliar to him as Dagmann's *Little Studies*. "How about Edith Sampson?" the collector counters, explaining she was a Manchester schoolteacher who produced as many as five hundred works including an opera and several symphonies, all unpublished and probably never performed, which he bought for fifty pounds from a junk shop, the price having mainly been for the trunk they were in. Conroy hasn't heard of her, nor the next name he is offered, a fusion of French and German whose second half rhymes with flower: Pierre Klauer.

"You have his manuscripts too?"

"Only a piano work. Quite remarkable, I think. Perhaps it might interest you."

Conroy detects that the collector is actually a dealer; their conversation is in danger of becoming a business transaction. "If you're looking to sell it…"

"I could send you a photocopy, I'd value your opinion. I believe he died young."

"How?"

"I'm still trying to find out. The piece is a mystery, too. I take it to be a sonata but on the title page it's called *Le Savoir secret.*"

The Secret Knowledge: an attractive name. For a moment Conroy fancifully imagines a come-back performance at the Wigmore Hall, a newspaper headline about a rediscovered masterpiece. "Do you have a card?"

The collector brings one from his wallet, bent and bruised from having been carried around too long. Conroy, lacking his reading glasses, holds it at a distance to see the name. "Claude Verrier. French? You don't have an accent."

"French descent but I pronounce my name the English way, it's simpler."

"Send me the Klauer sonata, I'd like to see it." Conroy gives his address, then it's time to say goodbye. Verrier leaves without an autograph.

At the restaurant it's Conroy, Tiff and a couple of others, local arts bureaucrats of some sort; pleasant and friendly, well used to dining out on other people's expenses. One is a charming self-described divorcee with a gleam in her eye that speaks of possibility, but she gets a call and has to leave. In the face of every diner Conroy sees the emptiness of pleasure and the inevitability of oblivion, and with each bottle of wine, flat-chested Tiff becomes more beautiful. Eventually they're all leaving, the handshakes on the pavement are brief and cursory, there's drizzle in the air and taxis have been spotted. Conroy says to Tiff, "Would you like to go for a drink?" She knows a good bar near his hotel, they talk there about music, the job market, basically nothing, and after a couple of whiskies he asks her to come back with him.

"I can't," she says simply, with the polite forcefulness of someone turning away a door-to-door salesman. He returns alone.

Lying clothed and shoeless on his mid-price bed sucking a miniature vodka from the minibar he feels glad she turned him down, regretful that he should have sunk so low. He's never been unfaithful to Laura in the years they've been together. In fact he wonders if loyalty is all that's left, dishonesty of a different kind.

He thinks of Edith Sampson and the trunk that must have been cleared out of her house by strangers after she died, the old lady's kitchen smelling of cat pee, her bedroom thick with dust, cupboards overwhelmed by ancient newspapers. The certainty of decay and the defiant will to write five hundred pieces of music only God would ever hear: the unshakeable faith of an artist in her own vision. He tries to replace the image with a more comforting one of Tiff's slender naked body but guesses she would have handled him in the same business-like way she settled the restaurant bill. For a young girl like her it's all so pragmatic and clearly defined, the future offering strength, not sadness. What future did Pierre Klauer have? Conroy guesses possible endings: doomed consumptive, spurned lover, uniformed skeleton in a trench. He imagines him a blood-streaked newborn spat into a midwife's hands, face pre-creased with inescapable fate.

He reaches to retrieve his phone from the pocket of his jacket, tossed on the chair beside the bed. It's late but he wants to hear Laura's voice, wants to say sorry for something, anything. He can't remember if she's meant to be back home by now or else still away on her assignment, some kind of environmental story she was investigating. Whenever she talks to him about practicalities and logistics he's got into the habit of tuning out.

Her phone can't be reached. Somewhere remote she was heading for, sheep and hills, poor signal. Probably sitting in front of a log fire in her B&B thinking what a shit he is. He's too old and scared to envisage a life alone without her, too weak, but he thinks of it, wondering if it might be best for both of them.

Stupid to imagine there was any chance with Tiff, she must have done it with artists far more successful than David Conroy. Her world is an open-plan promise of infinite efficiency but around its upper balcony stand an exiled crowd refusing to be ignored: the old and dead and forgotten. From beyond the ceiling of the hotel room, Pierre Klauer, Jan Timman, George DuFoy and a thousand others look down, angels of lowest rank, proletarians of artistic heaven, bathed in transcendent, annihilating light. Conroy's a minor pianist who had his chance but never hit the big time. That's why he has such affection for the little guys. When the woman told him that story about Alfred Brendel he wanted to puke, knew that if Brendel ever heard it he'd laugh his head off, wouldn't have a clue who she was. All of us, we're just performers.

When Conroy was Tiff's age he was being called one of Britain's most promising talents, his Shostakovich was "remarkable", he won a few prizes and thought, this is how it will always be, like this, forever, because this is what I deserve. Yet everything ends in a trunk on a skip, trash waiting to proclaim its true nature, yearning to liberate itself from illusion. His life's work has been the memory of his hands but it's the innate impulse of all things to be forgotten.

The Secret Knowledge. Verrier did a good pitch, mystery and secrecy are more attractive than fact. He gets up and takes another miniature, brandy this time, then lies back on the bed, eyes closed, watched over by the towering ranks of the eternal dead where Pierre Klauer stands, sombre and aloof. We are the unknown, he says, and you will join us.

1913

Ten days after Pierre's funeral, Yvette and her mother receive a visit from his cousin Gilberte; small, dark-eyed, dressed in black yet radiant with loss, her pale sharp features are determined to resist grief with dignity. Yvette follows little of the conversation while the three of them sit sorrowfully together, then Madame Courvelles excuses herself, leaving Yvette and Gilberte alone.

"I bring remembrances of Pierre." From her purse Gilberte extracts a small silver locket and a dried flower, the latter instantly comprehensible despite the wearying confusion of Yvette's mind. Pierre was wearing it when he was shot.

"I can't."

"Please."

Withered yet otherwise uncorrupted, the cattleya is like the remains of a saint; already, twirling it slowly in her fingers, Yvette envisages the jewelled reliquary that would be fit to house it. Before delivering the locket into Yvette's other hand, Gilberte opens it to reveal an encased curl of coal-black hair, and it is as if Yvette is reading everything in a book, viewing it in a carefully staged photograph, or from a vast distance through a telescope. She is not really here and none of this is happening. It is a fantasy – almost.

"I never saw him."

"I know that, Yvette."

"They wouldn't let me. Why wouldn't they let me see him?"

"Better to remember him in life."

"Not even in his coffin... Did you?"

"Let's not speak of it." Gilberte presses the locket into Yvette's palm. "Keep this and treasure it."

Yvette stares at the two lifeless souvenirs she holds, places them on the table beside her cooled teacup and asks again. "Did you see Pierre's body?"

"Yvette, you're only upsetting both of us."

"But did you?"

"No." Gilberte's porcelain face is impassive, her voice like the funeral oration Yvette hazily recalls that extolled with stoic finality Pierre's genius as musician and beauty as a man. "It was his parents' wish, you know that."

"A cruel wish."

She bristles. "Were it not for your mental condition I would find that remark inexcusable. Is your grief greater than theirs?"

"I only want to know why they hid him."

Gilberte, her errand already discharged, is like an actress impatient to reach the end of the scene when her role will be terminated and she can depart the theatre. "It's obvious why, Yvette, stop hurting yourself and others."

"They should have let me see him!"

So much weeping recently; Gilberte has become immune to it. "Control yourself and think what it must be like for them. You were spared and now you blame them for it."

"If I could have seen his face."

"He had no face!" Gilberte's outburst is like the gunshot itself. "Forgive me," she says softly.

Impervious to further hurt, her world having ended two weeks ago, Yvette remains numb. "I know how terrible he must have looked. But I should have been with him as he died, holding him in my arms. The crowd, the confusion, everyone saying different things…"

"You did nothing wrong."

"Or if they made a mistake. How can they be so sure it was Pierre?"

"You make it harder for yourself, Yvette."

"No," she says with sudden firmness, as if startled out of a daydream. "I've had enough of everyone trying to spare my feelings, treating me like a child. We were going to be married, he chose me as his wife."

"So you say…"

"It's true, Gilberte, and in my mind I'm his widow."

"In mind but not in fact." Gilberte's voice hardens with determination, the solidarity of a family that has resolved to close itself against disaster, intrusion, scandal. "His parents' wishes are final. I came in kindness to bring you these gifts from them, but what you say makes me doubt your gratitude. They have no obligation to you."

"I don't understand."

"They would prefer no further communication."

"I'm to be shut out?"

"You were never let in. You claim there was an engagement but there is no evidence of it, and Pierre's father would in any case not have given permission."

Yvette can barely feel the blow but she is aware of it, like witnessing an assault by one stranger on another. She feels pity of an abstract kind.

"I must leave," Gilberte says.

"I agree."

"I have other visits to make. Pierre had so many friends."

"Not all of them good. That's why he was murdered."

Gilberte rises brusquely. "Enough of this."

"But are the police still investigating? Why have they not come back to interview me again as they said?"

"The inquiry is no longer your concern."

"How can you possibly say that? You don't care, do you? None of you care. You simply want this terrible thing to go away – so you tell me to go. I won't be silent!"

"You know nothing, Yvette, and anything you say will only cause further anguish. If you try to spread rumours there will be consequences."

"Get out of here, damn you!"

Madame Courvelles re-enters just as Yvette is getting to her feet, the cousin stepping back in anticipation of being struck. The scene is undignified, ghastly. "Calm yourself!" Madame Courvelles cries as she rushes to embrace her daughter, both sobbing while Gilberte excuses herself and leaves.

The funeral, in Yvette's mind, was the wedding she and Pierre had planned, their union. Either she, too, is dead, or else the man is alive. Both possibilities exist for her with equal force and reality because around the incident in the park so much doubt adheres, obscuring truth, demanding faith. In the following days there is no further word from Pierre's family, from the police, or from anyone, as if all would prefer the couple never to have existed.

Leaving the house alone, intending to take some air, Yvette is met by the eyes of a brown-suited man coming along the pavement from the other direction who neatly raises his hat with a nod, as if he knows her and has the right to acknowledge it. She finds the gesture rude and unwelcome, fixes her line of sight ahead, but the man addresses her as she passes.

"Mademoiselle Courvelles."

She stops, turns and looks at him, silently demanding an explanation.

"You have my sincere condolences. Pierre was a fine man." The stranger must be only a few years older than she, but has a look of maturity and worldliness.

"You knew Pierre?"

His eyes roll in sad affirmation. "We were intimately acquainted. My name is Louis Carreau."

It means nothing to her. "Are you a musician?"

"A music lover but no expert. Pierre's circle was wide, it is not surprising if he never mentioned me. Though he spoke often of you."

She feels herself blush, and for the first time in weeks is aware of a smile on her lips.

"He loved you very much, mademoiselle. He told me... I shouldn't mention this."

"Tell me, please."

"He spoke of wanting to be with you forever."

Tears are in her eyes. "He is."

Carreau nods sorrowfully. "I suppose so."

Yvette can see he has the air of knowing more than he says. "What else did Pierre speak about?"

Monsieur Carreau suggests they walk together. "Pierre's interests were so varied, a conversation with him could be about art, philosophy, history."

"Or life," she recalls. "That most of all. The sheer joy of being in the world."

"Yes, mademoiselle, he had such hopes and ambitions, which is why I find the recent circumstances so mystifying and distressing."

They have reached the small gated garden that was her intended destination, but she continues past the entrance, still unsure of the man accompanying her. "I, too, am mystified, why anyone would do such a terrible thing to him." Carreau halts beside her; she sees pain on his face, its suddenness inexplicable. "You do know what happened, don't you?"

"I know what is asserted, mademoiselle, and that is what I find so incredible."

"That he was murdered?"

Carreau's expression alters once more. "You mean they didn't tell you?"

"What are you talking about?" She feels almost the same foreboding she experienced on the day it happened.

"I spoke carelessly, forgive me, it is of no consequence..."

"What should they have told me? I knew they were hiding something!"

Carreau looks skywards as though wishing reassurance of the earth's solidity. He speaks reluctantly, regretful both of the subject matter and of being forced to share it. His eyes when he levels them are so replete with earnest sympathy that he has the look of a professional mourner. "I have a friend in the justice ministry, I asked him to examine the papers relating to the case. There were witnesses to what happened. Mademoiselle, Pierre was not murdered..."

"My God, he's alive?"

Carreau shakes his head. "It was by his own hand."

She feels herself stagger; Carreau reaches to support her but quickly withdraws his arm when she shakes free. "Get away from me, you madman, or I shall call for help."

"I simply tell you what I know."

"This is all lies."

"You knew the family were concealing a fact more painful than the death itself, now you understand what it is. I am sorry to have brought you news of which you would have been better to have remained ignorant. I should bid you goodbye." He raises his hat again with the same polite self-assurance of his earlier introduction and is about to step away when Yvette, her thoughts restoring themselves to order, restrains him.

"How can they believe Pierre shot himself?"

"It is what the investigators have concluded, though they naturally wish to preserve the dignity of a high-ranking family."

"But it was only minutes after he proposed marriage to me."

Carreau's brow furrows in shared puzzlement. "He asked you that very day? Then the improbable becomes surely impossible."

Yvette's mind is racing. "We have to tell the police."

"It would not be a good idea."

"Or your friend in the ministry. Don't you see, Monsieur Carreau, there has been a terrible error, the police have got it wrong, he couldn't have done what they say."

Carreau sighs. "I've seen the papers, mademoiselle. I will not describe to you the detail with which one witness related what he saw, but I can tell you there is no doubt."

"He saw Pierre die?"

"He saw him point the gun between his eyes and pull the trigger."

Yvette covers her face.

"The witness saw the weapon go off, the wound it made. Death was instantaneous."

She is not too distraught to recognise the flaw in the story. "Where is this witness? Why should we believe him?"

"Others viewed less clearly but no less certainly. We know beyond question the manner of Pierre's death. It's the motive that I can't fathom. But for the police the case is closed, likewise for Pierre's family. It seems, mademoiselle, that you and I are the only persons interested in discovering the truth."

Finally she understands the reason why he has made himself known to her. "What should we do?"

"We can try to make enquiries of our own; but unless there is some further evidence, perhaps an unknown aspect of Pierre's life, a shadow that marred his happiness..." He stares penetratingly at her. "Can you think of anything at all?"

She says she can. The new friends, Pierre's disappearance, even the symphony; she tells Carreau everything, and finishes by bringing from inside the collar of her dress the fine gold chain that has been hanging round her neck, at the end of it a small key.

"This is what he gave you?" Carreau is transfixed as though by a priceless treasure; he peers closely at what she holds, longing to touch it. She removes the chain from her neck.

"Pierre was so insistent that I have it; at the time I thought... I don't know what I thought. Afterwards it seemed so inadvertently prophetic. Yet now..."

"Did you ever see the writing desk? Do you know where exactly it is situated in the house?"

"No... in his room I suppose. I can never go there, I wouldn't be admitted."

"But I can go." Carreau extends his palm. "I shall pay the parents my respects."

"And get Pierre's music? How?"

"I shall find a way, trust me."

She gives him the key, still on its fine chain, feeling as if she is giving up her own child, and in the moment when his fingers curl around the prize to take it from her, she is gripped again by doubt, and by the thought that in trying to save Pierre and his work she is really betraying him. "Give me something in return," she exclaims.

"You want payment? Some kind of pledge?"

"Only your word. Promise that you will bring it back to me, and the music. I've lost Pierre once already, I can't lose him again. Do this for me, Monsieur Carreau. Do it for our friend."

Carreau smiles thinly. "We shall both have what we want, Mademoiselle Courvelles. Trust me."

She feels she has made a terrible mistake; for some days afterwards there is no word from Carreau, she wonders if he is simply an unscrupulous music dealer willing to prey on a grieving woman in order to obtain a manuscript. A letter arrives, which she at first assumes must be from Carreau, though as soon as she begins to read, she realises it is from another.

My dear Mlle Courvelles,

I extend profound condolences and share your grief. Allow me to offer some recollections of our late friend, and believe me when I tell you, they are not without importance.

Pierre would frequently join me, along with several companions, at one or other of our favourite cafés, the popularity of each establishment being proportional to the leniency of its owner in allowing us credit. On one such occasion the topic for discussion was the nature of genius, there were six or seven of us round the table, our half-filled glasses politely and indefinitely preserved from being emptied, our impoverishment dignified by the richness of a conversation that brought Mozart, Michelangelo and Dante to a place favoured by thirsty dockers, as well as less honest members of the working class, male and female, of a kind you probably cannot imagine. I tell you this, mademoiselle, not so as to cast doubt on the honour and integrity of our friend, but merely to remind you that any young man of spirit and intelligence moves naturally, like a colourful fish in an aquarium, between the light of the surface, and the darker regions beneath.

A voice interrupted us. "Ha, genius!" We turned and saw at a neighbouring table a man alone, unshaven, dressed like an office clerk but so dishevelled as not to have been previously conspicuous. He was, in short, a drunk of the kind every watering hole knows, and before him on the table stood a glass of cognac. "You want to know about genius? I'll tell you about genius!"

We were all of us in good humour and ready for some sport. "Do tell, then," said one of us, an actor I shall call Duchêne. "But not for the price of another glass, since we don't have a sou between us!"

The drunk nodded with a bibulous smile, his eye gleaming. He rummaged inside his dirty jacket that I saw to be torn at the elbow, drew out a gold coin as bright as the filling in his tooth, and flicked it on his thumb, catching it in his hand. We waited for him to speak. He kept smiling, flicking.

"Well?" Duchêne said at last. "Is that all?"

We were about to turn from him when he stopped, reached out, and passed the coin to my friend. "Look carefully," he said.

Duchêne inspected the object, finding its brightness belied an unexpected antiquity. "It's from the eighteenth century." He looked up at the stranger. "Is it real?"

The man gave a shrug of indifference. "Depends what you mean. Study it closely."

We examined the coin, passing it among ourselves. It was

Pierre who spotted the pretence.

"This is fake," he declared. "It feels too light."

The man nodded. "It's made of glass. Belonged to my great-great grandfather who had it made in Switzerland – that and a thousand others."

"He was a counterfeiter?" one of us asked.

"We could use his talents!" another laughed.

Our companion allowed us our moment of frivolity. "He needed money in order to carry out a certain mission of what you might call a philosophical kind. This was the only way."

"Did he go to the gallows for it?" asked Pierre.

"No, he escaped, taking his precious papers with him."

Here, we recognised, was an artist of that all-too familiar kind, the bar-room raconteur. We had nothing to offer, we told him plainly, except our ears. Yet this seemed enough for him.

"My great-great-grandfather had acquired secret papers from a society formed by Jean-Bernard Rosier."

"Never heard of him," said Duchêne.

"No," said the man, "I wouldn't expect you to. He's not a name you'd ever have come across in respectable literature."

"Then what about disrespectable?"

"Perhaps," said the man, retrieving the coin that was handed back to him, its lustre less enticing now than the gleam of mystery. "I'm no Rosierist, I'm a humble engineer with too much of a taste for the ladies and the race track and the bottle. Yes, sirs, I'm a bum, I've not lived long and already I've wasted my life. But you gentlemen, you're interested in genius, and that's why I wanted to tell you my little story. Now I'd better leave."

"No, wait." It was Pierre who spoke. "Tell us more about Rosier's society. Was it political? A sort of freemasonry?"

"Best left alone," replied our companion, who, having

emptied his glass and seen that there was no prospect of replenishment, rose with only a little unsteadiness to his feet.

"Your name, monsieur?" It was I who asked.

"Minard."

All were ready to see the strange fellow leave, except Pierre. "I want to know more about Rosier," he said abruptly.

Minard eyed him with a sparkle of mischief and a shadow of enigma. "In that case you shall have to search hard, my friend, because I have told you all I can. Though if ever you go to the Blue Cat, especially on a Friday night, you might see me there."

Pierre warmed at the information. "Of course I know it – I've even played piano there to earn a few drinks."

Minard nodded with quiet satisfaction. "Then we shall meet again, my good pianist." And with that he left, the conversation quickly turned to matters of a kind I need not report to a lady such as yourself, and the toper with his fake coin was soon forgotten by all of us.

All, that is, except Pierre. It was many weeks later when he reminded me of the incident, and told me something else. He had been to the Blue Cat and had seen Minard not once but several times, plying him with cognac paid for by his sweet, nimble fingers; oh yes, mademoiselle, our beloved artist was playing music-hall songs or Schubert melodies in order that he could nourish the mercenary tongue of a fantasist. Let me assure you, moreover, that no other item attracted his attention in the insalubrious haunt he had come to patronise, save the smooth-tongued, fast-drinking engineer in his tattered coat, with his false gold piece flicking on his thumb.

Minard's ancestor, Pierre told me, had been entrusted with papers cursed by their own inflammatory outrageousness; the manifesto of a world transformed, the ground plan of a society

41

turned upside down by revolution, disdainful of logic as much as morality; the atlas of an alternative universe God rightly chose not to create. The Rosierists, if any still existed, were dedicated to its creation here on Earth.

My fear, when Pierre told me this, was not that he might fall into the hands of underground fanatics, since I felt sure those masked fiends lived only in Minard's fairy-tales. No, my fear was that Pierre was being seduced by lies, and that by dipping his toe into the mire his wily chum inhabited, he risked finding his foot stuck, then his leg and waist, until eventually his head would disappear into the filth. Forgive me for being so blunt, mademoiselle, but I have seen good men go bad before, and Pierre of all people must, I felt sure, be saved from such a fate.

I told Duchêne; we followed Pierre to the Blue Cat and saw him in conversation with three men – Minard was not among them. We had to be circumspect in our observation, but the briefest of glimpses was enough to satisfy me that these companions of his were no philosophers, no architects of Utopia. If there was anything I would have expected that group to plan, mademoiselle, it wouldn't be an ideal society – more like a terrorist atrocity. I tell you it as plainly as I can: they looked like assassins.

Soon afterwards Pierre disappeared. I knew at once that he must be in danger, though no one at the Blue Cat could tell me where he was, nor see reason for concern. One regular put a name to my description of the most memorable of the conspirators, a man whose long grey hair and blackened teeth identified him as LaForge, an old Blanquist, though it was said he had long ago given up revolution in favour of science, and was often heard expounding paradoxes about the laws of thermodynamics and the statistics of chance. A harmless crank, in other words, just like Minard – or so I thought, until

The Secret Knowledge

I heard of the ghastly incident at the park, when all my worst fears were confirmed.

This LaForge, I have learned, says each person's life is really a path through a branching labyrinth of possibilities; an idea that would surely have appealed to a sweet romantic such as Pierre, though we can only guess what other dark inferences the plotters must have reached from such outlandish premises. They are anarchists not just politically but also, even worse, intellectually, disdaining all logic and reason, and this, I maintain, is the explanation of Pierre's senseless death. They took an innocent man, seduced him with lies, put him up to some kind of spectacular outrage, a manifestation of their perverted philosophy. Now they laugh while we must weep.

The letter is unsigned; with its tales of hoaxes and delusions it has itself the stagnant air of fraudulence. Yvette has heard of troubled people who take sinister delight in taunting the bereaved; she worries that Louis Carreau might be another of those parasites. But then at last he calls on her, bringing both the precious key and the manuscript it has protected.

Madame Courvelles is with her when she receives him; Yvette explains to her the mission Monsieur Carreau has undertaken, and the sheets of music are passed between them for inspection.

"Are you a dealer?" Madame Courvelles asks the polite, smartly dressed young man who strikes her as looking more like a bank agent with good prospects.

"Neither a man of commerce nor at all musical," he tells her. "I'm a philologist."

That sounds good enough for Madame Courvelles; here is a decent fellow of the right age and class to lift Yvette out of her depression. Once she is satisfied of Carreau's honest principles, she allows them some time alone together.

"How ever did you get hold of it?" Yvette asks him at once.

"I bribed a servant. No one else knows of this work's existence."

The pages of music are in her hands, densely inscribed, impossible to imagine. Completely appropriate to the hieroglyphic enigma is the title: *The Secret Knowledge*.

"Pierre had many friends," she says. "Tell me what you know of them."

Despite this and all further oblique enquiries, applied with the subtle and well-aimed pressure one might employ against a stubborn limpet, Yvette is unable to lift from beneath Carreau's suave carapace the smallest evidence that he knows of Minard, Duchêne, LaForge, or anyone else mentioned in the letter. Pierre, she realises, lived in many worlds; he was like the comet that visits Earth briefly, gloriously, then flies to another sphere. Wait long enough, she thinks, and the comet may return.

"I owe you great thanks for the service you have done me, Monsieur Carreau. At the very least, I should repay your expenses."

With a wave of his hand, a whiff of cologne, he dismisses such concerns. "I did it for Pierre, and for yourself. I know how much he loved you – and I can easily see why." A new gravity attaches itself to him. "You must be very careful."

"What do you mean?"

"The forces that surrounded our friend were powerful and dark. Conceal the music score and keep it safe, a precious relic, show it only to trusted eyes and say he gave it to you before he died."

"Of course, I shall never allow myself any indiscretion that would compromise you…"

"Allow me the honour of being your protector."

Though said sincerely it sounds improper. "I'm not aware I require any protection of a kind my family cannot provide."

"I'm sure Pierre would have said the same thing, but consider what happened to him."

"You think I'm in danger? The police should be told."

"That would not be wise. I have taken a personal risk on your behalf, as you kindly acknowledge, and all I ask in return is that you do not shun my offer of assistance, for this is a matter of common concern and mutual interest. Through involvement in those sinister powers that killed Pierre, we may both find ourselves placed in danger."

Had she not previously read the letter about which she remains silent, she might have dismissed Carreau's words entirely. Instead she understands their significance, coded like the score she holds, and thus it is in a mood of foreboding that she concludes this interview with the man who will become her husband.

Chapter Two

Paige is on her way to her first piano lesson with Mr Conroy when on the pavement she sees a dead bird. Dark feathered, blackbird or crow (she doesn't know the difference), the creature lies huddled at the foot of a garden wall like an expired vagrant, head askew, glazed eye half-open. She feels momentary disgust, then pity. Do birds die in mid-air and fall to the ground? Or do they sense the approaching end, huddle down and expire? Paige is twenty years old but imagines herself suddenly ancient and alone, flying over rooftops, her heart abruptly stopping, air rushing past.

After the miscarriage she decided she would go against her parents' wishes, give up the English degree she had started and study piano full-time instead. She'll be left heavily in debt and with little prospect of a career, but she's determined that as long as she has wings she'll use them.

She's heard that Mr Conroy can be difficult, he wasn't on the panel when she did the college audition and really she doesn't need to impress him, she's been accepted on the course and his job is to help her improve. But she wants to do well. She turns from the dead bird and walks on. Children will find

It, poke it with sticks; at night it will be removed by a fox or rat, or else simply rot there, eaten by maggots.

At the hospital she told them she hadn't realised she was pregnant, it was still so early, but she'd felt unwell with pain in her lower back, then it came out in the toilet, a formless lump like a pink cabbage stalk, she had to fish it out and couldn't believe what it was until she saw fingers, a tiny red-lined fist. They asked if she'd like to have counselling and she said no, then they took the cabbage stalk and put it in an incinerator.

Outside the college there's another protest. Half a dozen students are demonstrating against capitalism, cuts, whatever. They're standing on the broad steps of the pompous Victorian building, politely gathered to one side so as not to cause an obstruction.

"Hi, Paige," says a skinny guy in red-tinted shades and a Hollister beanie, his placard painted with large lettering. She smiles as she goes past to the revolving door. Can't remember his name.

The lobby's busy, it's changeover and people are heading for their next class, she pauses to let a chattering crowd go by and finds herself beside a display case, relics glorifying past successes, famous alumni. A century-old sepia photograph shows the entrance hall she stands in, same ornate arch and marble staircase but with an earlier generation of musicians posing smartly on it, young like her yet all now dead. Crossing the lobby, her view captures a boy reading the notice board, another with his cello case, two girls texting silently side by side, a seated man wearing an eye-patch. On the stairs there's a fallen sheet of paper, a page of manuscript lost from a composition assignment. She considers picking it up, handing it in, but hurries on.

She finds the room, no one's there, she waits at the door

until he arrives, brusque Mr Conroy carrying a bundle of music scores. Tall, dark haired, not bad looking for his age, but tired. He unlocks the door and waves her inside, tells her to sit at the further of two grand pianos whose keyboards stand side by side like office desks. He isn't strong on introductions or small-talk, hasn't even confirmed who he is, but this is the one who will train her, a man with medical detachment, polite, distant. This, she thinks, must be what she needs. The room's plain white walls, geared to acoustics rather than visual appeal, add to an atmosphere of scientific enquiry.

"How long have you been playing?"

"I started when I was four."

"How long is that?"

"Sixteen years."

"And what have you done?"

She tells him about the lessons, certificates and school competitions, her schedule of practice and the degree course she gave up because music is all that matters to her. He's more interested in knowing who's been teaching her, he doesn't recognise any of the names.

"Play something," he instructs, then goes to stand at the window, looking out while she begins her audition piece, Chopin's *Barcarolle*. She's unfazed by his manner and performs perfectly, though after a while he suddenly makes her stop. "What chord was that?"

She has to think for a moment. "A sharp major."

"Why?"

She doesn't understand. "What do you mean, why?"

"What's it for?"

Another moment's thought. "It's a modulation to D sharp minor."

"And when you switched course, was that a transposition

from one place to another, or did it mean something?"

He's saying that she plays without meaning. She thinks of the dead bird.

"Can you give me some Beethoven?" he asks, and she offers the 'Waldstein' Sonata. This time he lets her play for longer, she feels she's doing well, but the question haunts her: why? And always at the corner of her vision she can see him gazing through the window, as though asking that same question.

Something gets made by accident, a pink lump of nothing, then it's burned in an incinerator and becomes another kind of nothing. Notes of music are written, performed, vanish like smoke. As she reaches the end of the exposition Conroy interrupts, "That's enough." She stops, waiting for his opinion, pained by the silence that follows. Then he turns and tells her, "That was good."

She feels a rush of relief and gratitude.

"But we'll have a lot of work to do. How did you first encounter the piece? Playing or hearing?"

"CD."

"Who?"

"I don't remember."

"When I was ten my parents gave me the LP by Wilhelm Kempff."

In his expression she sees something of the proud and lonely boy he must have been.

He says, "First time I heard it I thought: this can't possibly be right, this strange sound starting to come out of the record player, not a tune but a single quiet chord repeated again and again. I even thought the needle might be jumping. You see how important it is, that first moment?"

He sits at the other piano, deposits his scores on the closed lid then plays the opening, more slowly and softly than Paige did, making it seem unexpectedly mysterious. He stops suddenly and says, "What does it make you see?"

She doesn't know how to answer, the picture in her mind is the studio of her former music teacher Mrs Fleming, heavy rain outside, her period that was starting. "A river," she suggests.

"Adorno said it made him think of knights in a forest."

She doesn't know who he's referring to, the puzzlement on her face must be evident.

"You haven't heard of Theodor Adorno? German philosopher and musician, Thomas Mann's friend." She's still blank, and Conroy says, "When I was a student we got a lot of Adorno, one of the lecturers was really big on Marxist philosophy. You see, Adorno could still hold on to his childhood idea, even when he was reflecting on Beethoven as an adult. Two completely different views of the same object. That's how you can keep it new. Your playing doesn't sound new, it sounds rehearsed. Too loyal to the score. Have you got a piano at home?"

"Only an electronic one. I'm in a flat."

"Do you live alone?"

The question feels abruptly personal. "No. But my flatmate's mostly away."

"I got back from touring and found my partner had walked out."

Paige shifts uncomfortably. She says nothing.

"Really I'd been alone all the time. Pianists, we're solitary by nature."

"Not necessarily."

He looks surprised. "Maybe you don't feel it yet. You will, if you carry on. But we need to strengthen the left hand. And the pedalling was all over the place." He's looking at her arms and legs, dissecting her. "What's your ambition?"

"To play better."

"Why?"

"It's what I love."

His brow rises. "The word amateur means doing it for love; this place is meant to train professionals."

"I don't care about that."

"Love can break your heart."

"It's worth the risk."

He smiles. "I like that. Too many artists don't take risks, they find something they're good at and keep doing it the same way forever." He stands up. "Play me something you love."

She offers a piece from Janacek's suite *On An Overgrown Path*. It will always be connected in her mind with the cabbage stalk, the woman at the hospital, the smell of the corridors. In the whole of her body she can feel the meaning of the music, he lets her play to the end and she expects him to pass judgment but instead after a pause he says, "Did you say you studied physics?"

"No, English."

"I was sure you said physics."

It's as if he wasn't listening. She wonders if he's making some kind of point.

He tells her, "I met a physics student the other day and asked him about Schrödinger's cat. You know, the thing that's neither dead nor alive, or both at once. The student said, maybe we're all inside the box. What do you think he meant?'

"I've no idea."

"Probably nothing. Why did you choose the Janacek?"

"Because I love it. That's what you asked for."

"You played well."

She hopes he'll elaborate but instead he wants to go back to the 'Waldstein', there are passages he asks to hear again,

51

he makes her play them repeatedly, demonstrating at his own keyboard what he wants her to do. Imagine you're singing, he tells her, think where you would take a breath, what the words might be, which syllables you would stress. Think of the audience who need to feel as if all of this is coming into being right now, in this exact moment. Trying to follow his instructions, struggling against the differing will of her own fingers, she wonders if there will ever be an audience. For half an hour they work on a single short section until Conroy says he can see she's tired, they should finish with something else. From his pile of scores he lifts some loose sheets and passes them to her, photocopied pages of handwritten music. The notes are small but neatly formed, the tempo heading is 'grave'.

"Try this."

"What is it?"

"A slow movement by someone you've never heard of. Take a minute then start whenever you're ready." He gets up and returns to the window, looking out while she picks up the single line of the opening, and she wonders if his point now is to make her think about that first instant when everything is unknown and genuinely new, a moment always about to be lost. It's a peculiar melody, a sinuous curve in the right hand, punctuated by unexpected angles. She supposes it to be a theme that will be developed or varied, but the following full chords introduce a new, unrelated idea. The harmonies feel wrong, she's sure she must be making mistakes, misreading the tiny accidentals; she constantly expects to be told to stop, but he lets her continue. He said it took only a few seconds before the 'Waldstein' made sense to his childhood ear, but this piece is different, an object on which she can't sustain any view, its shape constantly altering. She passes through flashes of beauty, transitory episodes of rich sonority, but set among formless progressions of bewildering complexity. And then the single line reappears, only this time it's different, the corners have moved.

"Stop there," he says gently. "What's your opinion?"

"I couldn't get it. I'd need to play it a few times."

"When do you think it was written?"

There was something in it that reminded her of Messiaen. "Nineteen sixties?"

"Go back fifty years. Pierre Klauer was a student at the Paris Conservatory with a great future ahead of him. Shortly after writing this he shot himself."

"I sensed a strangeness in the music."

"A man who's talented, confident, yet he's about to commit suicide. A contradiction." He shows her another of the photocopied sheets. "You see what he called it? *The Secret Knowledge*."

"The secret is why he killed himself."

"The secret is the music. I want you to learn the whole of the movement for next time. And I want you to keep hold of the confusion, don't try to resolve it, because I can tell you now, there won't be an answer, there never is. Art is always inconsistent."

She came to this first lesson with the hope of being praised and complimented; instead she leaves still wondering if Mr Conroy thinks she has any talent at all. When she goes downstairs she sees that the dropped sheet has been removed, a different crowd of people fills the lobby, the protesters have gone for lunch. But on her way home, the bird is still there, exactly where it lay.

Her flat is on the first floor, she splits the rent with Nathalie who works shifts as a nurse and is mostly at her boyfriend's;

the couple below leave early for work every morning and make no noise. Paige might as well be living alone, though she still chooses the further isolation of headphones while practising. The Klauer piece will be a chore to learn, she's not sure whether Mr Conroy will expect her to play it from memory. She wonders if he'll ever make a pass at her, and how she'd feel about it.

In a couple of days it's coming together, she knows the movement's shape, even if she still doesn't understand it. There are two main themes, she realises, presented alternately in different ways, together with other material that seems more random. Does she like the piece? The question is irrelevant: it's simply there, and she has to learn it.

She meets her friend Ella for coffee and tells her about the college. Ella wants to know if there are any good-looking boys on the course. They're in Starbucks, a new branch only recently opened, Paige wonders what the place used to be, how long it will survive in this latest incarnation, thinking it while Ella talks about something else, her freshly dyed red hair making her pretty face look even paler than usual, energised with transitory importance. Paige gets a call on her phone, looks at the screen and doesn't recognise the number, puts the phone to her ear and Ella falls silent.

"Paige, it's David Conroy."

At first she can't connect the name with any person, she's so surprised to be called by her tutor.

"There's something we need to discuss. Could we meet?"

Her confusion must be visible to Ella, who can hear it's a man at the other end.

"I have to ask you to return the score I gave you. I'll explain when I see you. Things are stranger than I thought."

1919

Scotland

John Quinn waits at the gate of Russell Engineering on a dark
January evening as the workers emerge, caps pulled low, coats
buttoned against the frigid air. "*Advance*, one penny!" Quinn
shouts, brandishing a bundle of printed pages in his upheld
hand. "Support the campaign for a forty-hour week." Most
ignore him as they pass, too tired to comment. A few tell him
to be off; their union, like most in Scotland, has already voted
against – why should they heed this lad or his newspaper? But
one man stops.

"I'll buy a copy." The accent is foreign.

"A penny."

He searches his pocket. "*Merde*. Only three farthings."

"Have it for two."

"You should come on Friday when we have our pay
packets." He takes the paper, pays his coins and reads the

masthead. "*Advance*. I like that. I'm a believer in progress."

Quinn barely notices the last of the men trudging indolently behind the stranger, his features strikingly shadowed in the lamplight. "You're French?"

"I was."

"How do you come to be here?"

"Events occurred." The newspaper consists of a single spread the Frenchman opens and quickly peruses. "You have written this?"

"There's a group of us."

"Communists?"

"Socialists."

He nods pensively. "I should like to meet your group."

Quinn is delighted. "You're most welcome…"

"But I think your newspaper is very bad," he says, dismissively folding it. "And you wasted your time trying to sell it here. You don't mind my being blunt, do you?"

"Of course not," Quinn says, humbled.

"In France we have had a little more experience of revolution. You could say that along with women and wine it is a national speciality." The stranger laughs, nudges his new friend, and Quinn is bathed by the warmth of exotic lands. "My name is Pierre Klauer." Their introductory handshake is like a pact.

"Come for tea," Quinn says abruptly, almost surprising himself with his own hospitality.

"I should like that, whenever is convenient for you."

"Come now. Unless you need be somewhere else."

Pierre shrugs affably. "I have no prior engagement."

The factory gate is quiet, the winter evening cold; there is no further cause for formality. "Let's go then," says Quinn. He's parked his bike against a nearby wall; he pushes it while

Pierre carries the satchel of unsold newspapers. Quinn asks how long the Frenchman has been in Scotland.

"I arrived before the war, unfortunately."

"You'd have preferred to be with your own people?"

"I was imprisoned by yours. My father was born in Germany; the one thing I have from him is his surname."

"I'm sorry."

"It's not your fault."

"What was prison like for you?"

"It gave me time to think."

Leaning on the handlebars of the bike he wheels, Quinn agrees earnestly. "Plenty of time, certainly." They take the path beside the river, poorly lit and muddy in parts. "Where do you live?"

"At a lodging house near Logie Colliery. And you?"

"Not far, in Mossmount."

"Ah, the respectable part of town. Then you're what they call 'posh'?"

Quinn laughs, unsure if Pierre is being naive or ironic. "My father's a doctor, a very good one and a brilliant man, though highly traditional in his politics. Like you, I've inherited nothing but a name. He says I've brought shame to it."

"He lets you remain beneath his roof, that shows how much he loves you."

"He needs me and my sister to look after him since mother fell ill." Quinn catches himself. "How vain of me to expound on my own circumstances. I fear I may bore you." He feels a comforting hand on his arm.

"It makes me happy that you speak freely."

They walk in darkness; beyond the river's murmur the town is alive only with the distant sound of workers retreating to home or pub.

Pierre asks, "Are you employed?"

"I'm a student."

"I thought you might be."

"Started in medicine, failed my exams, simply couldn't take it in. Father suggested law but that was no better. Then the war…"

"You fought?"

"No," says Quinn, slowing to a halt. "You told me honestly about your misfortune – it's one I shared."

"Prison?"

"I was called up but declared myself a pacifist. Father got me out, the lawyers argued that as a medical student I should never have been conscripted. So it was back to anatomy, and now it's all over I can change subject again. Or to hell with it."

"It was brave of you, refusing to enlist. For me there was no choice."

"It wasn't hard, telling the board I wouldn't fight for capitalism. It was when I heard of so many friends dying that I felt ashamed."

"We must put the past behind us," Pierre says soothingly. "For everyone this is the start of a new life. I began at the factory only two weeks ago."

"And in France? What did you do there?"

"I told you," says Pierre, "let's not dwell on the past."

They take the lane leading to Mossmount and come eventually to a street of dignified stone houses with neat gardens. Quinn's front door opens before they reach it; a pretty red-haired young woman stands waiting.

"Hello, Jessie," Quinn says, stooping to kiss her cheek, then looks over his shoulder. "Pierre, this is my wee sister."

Enchanté, mademoiselle."

She smiles nervously, pleasurably, looking to her brother

for further explanation, her face like that of a child seeing Santa Claus, but Quinn only asks, "Is father here?"

"In the front room." Jessie offers to take the men's coats for them as they step inside.

"Pierre's having his tea here, can you manage that?"

"I expect so."

A gravelly voice calls. "Is that you, Johnny?"

"Yes, father. We have a guest I'd like you to meet."

"Come here, then."

Dr Quinn sits in an armchair near the curtained window, a book open on his lap. Freckled, bald, eyebrows grey and shaggy, his old face is ruddy in the firelight. "I won't stand, if you don't mind."

"Pierre Klauer, sir, at your service."

"Is that a Belgian name you've got?"

"French, sir."

"Then what would you prefer, whisky or brandy?"

"I like whisky very much."

"See to it, Johnny, will you? Only a wee drop of water for me, mind. Have a seat, Pierre. I've been chuckling at this book, very droll. *The Man Who Was Thursday*. You know Chesterton?"

"No, sir."

"I suppose not." The doctor quickly finds another topic. "Most appalling what the Hun's done to your country."

"A tragedy."

"How did the land of Beethoven ever go so wrong, can you tell me that? Do you like music, Pierre?"

"In fact I do."

"I used to sing often when I was younger. Handel's *Messiah*, they have it in France I expect." He takes the glass his son offers and stares at it disapprovingly. "Are we running short?

What's your profession, Pierre?"

"He just started at Russell, father."

The son's interruption makes Dr Quinn stare from one man to the other as though wondering where the next voice might come from. "An engineer? That's very fine. The world needs engineers. Was that your father's profession too?"

"My father built his fortune from arms factories in Germany."

A stunned blinking of Dr Quinn's grey eyes. All he can manage after a moment is, "I see."

"But you've broken with your father, haven't you?" John asks uncertainly.

Pierre nods. "You could say I broke with everything." He looks straight at Dr Quinn. "Would you prefer me to leave, sir?"

"Of course not."

"I can't help the way my father became rich. I've disowned him."

The doctor pensively rubs the indentations of his crystal glass. "Very sad. Though under the circumstances, clearly appropriate." He again looks from one man to the other. "Johnny, how did you two meet? How long have you been acquainted?"

"A while," Pierre answers quickly. There is a palpable air of something unstated; John does nothing to contradict a lie he finds strangely pleasant.

"Pierre was interned as an alien."

The doctor's eyebrows sink with sorrowful understanding. So that's it: prison-mates. Best not discuss further. "You're having tea with us?"

"If I may."

"Jessie should have sorted it by now, let's go through."

In the dining room the table is set, the meal is ready.

"This looks wonderful," Pierre says approvingly, making Jessie blush as she comes from the kitchen with a serving ladle.

"If I'd known we'd have a guest…" She sits down without completing her sentence, toying instead with her hair.

"Will you write a wee note for mother tonight?" Dr Quinn asks, and she nods. He explains to Pierre, "My wife's in a sanatorium. Her lungs, you understand. My eyes aren't as good as they used to be so Jessie takes care of letters."

"I wish your wife good health, sir."

"We pray for her."

Jessie crosses herself; no one else cares to repeat the gesture. Pierre is invited to serve himself the stew steaming in a casserole whose size emphasises the frugality of the contents. He takes a spoonful.

"Go on, lad," the doctor urges. Slices of buttered bread lie on a plate beside a pot of tea. John Quinn looks at his sister and sees how she stares at the stranger, as much in awe as John himself. Taking a piece of bread, Pierre appears perfectly at ease.

"Are you Parisian?" Jessie asks.

"I was."

"It must be so beautiful. Will you go back?"

"I think not."

She, too, catches the seductive aroma of secrecy. Surely a woman, she guesses. "Do you like Scotland?"

"Certainly."

"What in particular?"

Pierre smiles. "Not the weather, of course. But the landscape, the colours."

"The people?"

"Yes, very friendly and welcoming. And the history."

"I love history," she says quickly. "When I was at school it was always my favourite subject."

"But we learned so little of it," John interrupts. "Real history, I mean. It was only kings and queens and battles and treaties."

His sister's mystified. "What else could it have been?"

"The lives of ordinary working folk."

She laughs. "We know enough about that already."

"I don't know that you do."

Dr Quinn intervenes. "Stop bickering, you two."

"It's just a discussion," John says. "Pierre, you agree with me, don't you? The history books are written by the ruling class and only tell their side of the story."

All look to Pierre for an answer. He pouts thoughtfully as he considers the question. "There is always another side to everything."

"Exactly!" says John.

"Even in the stories of the ruling class there may be something worth hearing." He looks at Jessie while he speaks, and John begins to wonder if his new friend is really a socialist after all.

There is a loud knock at the front door; Jessie goes to answer.

"History is a science," John says in a low voice that is almost belligerent. "They don't teach the laws of history at school…"

But before he can elaborate further, Jessie comes back. "Father, there's been an accident at the foundry."

Dr Quinn shoots to his feet with sudden youthfulness. "Well then, I'd better see what some poor fool's gone and done to himself."

He goes to the hallway followed by his daughter, leaving

John to pick up a theme he is unable to relinquish. "You agree, I suppose?"

"About the laws of history?"

"Otherwise I can't understand why you might want to help with *Advance*. Why you stopped at the gate to talk to me, why you came here."

Pierre considers the matter and in the gaslight looks almost beautiful. "Why?" he says. "Because history demands it. Yes, there are laws, John, as powerful as gravity, but they're not for everyone to learn."

"You don't believe in educating the proletariat?"

"I'm not a Marxist."

"Then what the devil are you? How can I know you're not some management spy?"

"I suppose you can't. I should leave."

"No. But I don't know if I should trust you."

"You don't have to. I wish to help, that's all. Give me some of your newspapers and I'll sell them at the works."

"You could be sacked."

"I'm not afraid. I'll write for you, speak at your meetings, whatever you require. And if you like, you can always assume that I'm a spy. That way you'll never tell me anything you wouldn't want the enemy to hear."

Jessie is closing the front door on her father, soon to come back. "I can't work you out at all," John says to Pierre.

"Then don't try. Let's simply be friends."

As Jessie enters she sees their handshake, feels the eerie solemnity of the alliance. That night, writing to her ailing mother, she makes no mention of it.

The newspaper is produced at Maclean's printing works, whose usual output is headed stationery or calling cards for inhabitants of the town able to afford such tokens of prestige, though lately it has been matter of another kind that has rolled from the presses, the printing shop serving as editorial office for as long as the *Advance* committee can keep up regular payments and avoid prosecution. Ten days after first meeting Pierre, John Quinn is there amid the rhythmic clatter of the machinery, looking at the freshly produced sheet being held up for his perusal.

"You've misspelled committee."

"Eh?" Angus Blackhorn, sleeves rolled dirtily up his ink-blackened arms, peers where Quinn indicates, and discovers the misprint. "Damnation!"

"We can't let it go like that."

"What, re-do the whole bloody run?"

"Or correct them by hand."

"Stay all night, then," Blackhorn bawls irritatedly above the mechanical din. "You and that damn idiot Harry Orr."

"We have to do something about it."

"Smash his bloody teeth's what I'll do when he gets here. Calls himself a proof reader and can't spell committee."

At the far end of the room, typesetter Malcolm Baine is going about his work, glad to be beyond range of Blackhorn's verbal shrapnel, though not for long.

"Aye, you as well, Baine, at least Orr's got a bloody mouth. How did you not see it? 24-point headline!"

Quinn attempts diplomacy. "It's nobody's fault, Angus." This only lights another fuse.

"It's everybody's fucking fault! Orr and Baine and you too. All the decent men got blown to buggery, that's the problem."

Quinn's ears are hurting, he carries the still-wet sheet to the adjoining room where Joe Baxter, sitting peacefully and caressing warm tea in a tin mug, looks up and asks, "What's the matter with you, then?" When Quinn shuts the door on the noise and tells him, he laughs. "Committee? You reckon there's five people in Kenzie know how to ruddy spell?"

Quinn pulls a chair beside the old man, spreads the sheet on the table and reads the rest of it, fearing further errors. But the date and venue of the public meeting are correctly given, the arguments in favour of a forty-hour working week appear in order. From the page, words come forward for inspection: industry, grievance, solidarity, participate; stepping out of context of neatly printed lines and standing to attention looking proud, obedient, doomed.

"Discovered any more?" Joe Baxter asks after a while.

"Not yet."

"When you've been in the trade as long as me you know how little it matters to anyone else, it's only ourselves who notice." Quinn keeps reading but Baxter, on his break, is in conversational mood. "We like to do a perfect job, that's natural. Nothing worse than slack work, makes me irate when I see a badly set line in a newspaper, even books these days are in a poor state and not only because of the war. Young ones now have no self respect, not like when I started. Do your shift and draw your wage, that's their way, and never mind the task in hand. It's a sad business. I wouldn't want to be your age now, John, not with the way the world's going. Soon you'll all be pushing buttons ten hours a day."

Quinn looks up. "Not on basic pay though."

Baxter laughs and raises his mug. "A toast to the revolution and home rule."

The door opens before they can discuss it further and Pierre Klauer briskly enters, cheerfully depositing his canvas bag on the table. Quinn moves his page clear of the intrusion.

"I sold nearly all of mine today," Pierre announces, opening the bag to show how few copies of *Advance* lie bent beside a bundle of greasy brown paper containing the remains of his dinner.

"Well done young Frenchman," Baxter declares, having grown paternally fond of Pierre in the short time they have been acquainted.

"There'll be more for you to sell tomorrow," Quinn says with what both other men register as a scowl.

"He's vexed over a misprint," Joe Baxter explains.

"Only that? If I worried about every mistake I made in life then my hair would have turned white by now."

"It's in a headline," says Quinn. "It looks foolish."

Pierre removes his bag to see the page pushed beneath his gaze, his lips quivering as he reads. Eventually he says, "I find nothing wrong."

Quinn points. "Committee."

"I would never have known."

"You see, John?" says Baxter. "Let it pass. Angus has enough on his hands out there without getting the dictionary thrown at him."

Pierre agrees. "I can tell he's in one of his black moods." Angus was invalided back from Passchendaele and all who knew him agree he has never been the same since. Pierre remarks on the printed notice. "The meeting is so soon."

"It's the only date I could get for the hall."

"No use advertising it here, there should be posters and leaflets."

"That's too much to ask of Maclean."

"Then your meeting will be a failure, John. I should worry about that instead of a spelling mistake."

If this is meant as a provocation it fails. "I know how to run the campaign, Pierre."

"And I am trying to help."

"Then sell as many of these as you can tomorrow."

Pierre is immovable. "I cannot sell to men who gave me money today."

"It's a petty sum."

"Not when doubled in a single week. I shall give copies gratis and ask my comrades to distribute them. Otherwise the meeting will be a waste of time."

John stares at the table, bridling at this challenge to his authority while doubting his ability to exert it. He says quietly, "Do you wish to help or do you prefer to be in charge?"

"What?"

"This is a great deal of work, Pierre, I'd happily give it to someone else."

Baxter gets up, puts his half-empty mug beside the sink, and goes back to the printing room.

Pierre asks, "Who will speak at the meeting?"

"I've contacted a few people."

"You've left it all too late. This needs thought and planning, it takes time. If you want to persuade the workers of this town to become involved in national action then you have only one opportunity to do it, one moment when you can win their hearts. One test that you either pass or fail."

The words sting Quinn's heart; he looks sadly at Pierre. "I always fail."

"That's not true at all."

"How my father will laugh." He bites at his lip. "What are we to do?"

"It's quite simple," says Pierre. "Let me be the main speaker. I promise you that what I say will be worth hearing."

Chapter Three

Samuel Johnson said that if you want to be an artist then be a mediocre one, since the public for the most part have mediocre taste. Arriving home from his concert tour Conroy considers this observation as true nowadays as it was in the eighteenth century. The last of his three appearances was part of "Tune Inn", a crassly named festival of music and fine food put together by some kind of local development agency in association with various media and sponsorship partners. Conroy never figured out the details and honestly didn't care, he was there to give the same programme he'd offered at his other two engagements: Beethoven's Opus 26, Firelli's *Dance Suite*, some Chopin mazurkas, Schumann's *Kreisleriana*. He got there and found he was up against Paul Morrow, they'd put the two pianists head to head, the timings overlapped so it was impossible for anyone with a genuine taste in art rather than salad dressings to attend both recitals. Morrow, half Conroy's age, is the latest photogenic long-haired wunderkind, the press love how he plays in jeans and says he doesn't mind if people talk during the performance, they do it at rock concerts after all, so why not classical ones? When Beethoven was debuting his own works, people would drink and talk.

Yes, thinks Conroy, and Beethoven fucking hated it. He unlocks his front door, deactivates the burglar alarm and sees the mail piled on the floor, he thought Laura would be back already but she must still be away on her assignment. He's had no more texts, hasn't been able to speak to her since that last argument. Among the junk mail there's a large envelope with a handwritten address, he takes it to the kitchen and opens it after he's put on the kettle. The collector he met at the second performance, Verrier, has sent a photocopy of the sonata he mentioned.

Conroy's parched, makes some tea and sits at the kitchen table. Showed up at Tune Inn and the green room was a marquee with rugs and sofas, ethnic finger food, crew of enthusiastic helpers fresh out of university. One of them said come and meet Paul Morrow who was sitting holding court with a glass of white wine in his hand, Conroy couldn't tell if the ongoing repartee was a press interview or regular conversation. Of course he didn't want to come and meet bloody Paul Morrow.

He quickly looks at the Klauer score and reads the accompanying letter from Verrier who's been doing some research and says the composer died from a gunshot wound in a Paris park in 1913, reported in the press as a tragic accident, probably a polite way of saying suicide. Klauer's handwritten notation on the photocopied sheets is neat and readable, first movement looks interesting, perhaps a touch of Busoni about it. Again the tantalising vision of a come-back concert, media interest. Forget the music; the troubled young genius blew his brains out and the world unjustly forgot him, that's a story.

Morrow, unshaven in baggy blue pullover, was telling his little entourage about his plan to do the complete *Well-Tempered Clavier* at Heathrow airport. "Like, you can buy your duty free, listen to some Bach, whatever." The juvenile assistant with a Tune Inn tee-shirt did the introductions, Morrow didn't bother getting up but stretched an arm in languorous handshake. He'd obviously never heard of Conroy, had no idea he might face any kind of competition for audience-share that afternoon, knew in any case it would be no contest. Wine-glass in hand, Morrow generously asked about Conroy's programme, nodding with approval. "Great line-up, I've never heard of the Firelli, that sounds really cool. I'd love to hear your gig, man, it's fucking nuts the way they scheduled it. Wonder if they could change the timings? And *Kreisleriana*, that's wicked."

The Tune Inn organisers hadn't stopped to ask themselves how two guest artists might feel about being made to clash, they had thought only about abundance of consumer choice: a jazz quartet in a kitchenware promotion, Mongolian folksong next to a lecture on Italian wine, some Debussy for dessert; or if not that, then an entirely different permutation from the menu. Morrow was inter-changeable with a TV chef, Conroy with a jar of mustard. He asked Morrow, "Have you ever read *Kreisleriana*?"

A double-take, like it was some new kind of street-talk that needed decoding. "You mean played it?"

"It's a book by E.T.A. Hoffmann."

"No shit."

Morrow looked genuinely interested to learn more but his female minder interrupted to say they needed to go outside for a photo shoot and that was the end of the conversation. Instead Conroy had to continue it inside his own head, telling the departed Morrow that the book features a musician completely opposed to false reputation, the shallowness of mass taste and received opinion; a person living for art in a world that recognises only commercial value, therefore considered mad.

The Secret Knowledge

Conroy sips his tea, thinks about unpacking. He used to keep a bag permanently ready for concert travel, these days he doesn't need to. Eventually he lifts his case from the hall and takes it to the bedroom, some of the shirts have remained unworn and can be hung before he dumps the rest in the washing machine. He opens the wardrobe. Half the space inside is empty. Laura's clothes are gone.

First thought that hits him: we've been burgled. Next: why did she take all her clothes for a trip of a few days? Then at last the truth, at least twenty minutes before he finally accepts it, once he's established that she's removed not only her clothes but every item she owns, every ornament and photo, cleared herself completely out of his house, his life, told him unarguably that it's over. And he realises that it was already over when he left for the tour, finished even before then. It was over from the first moment they met. Their entire relationship was between two people destined to part.

Everything really happens long before it becomes fact; public knowledge is invariably the last to arise. How long was Laura planning her escape, when did she decide on the form of her exit? Conroy's still asking himself the question hours later, the whisky bottle almost empty, something happening on television that he doesn't feel the need to comprehend. This is how all things conclude: badly, without resolution. He knew it when he was stupidly trying to get off with that girl after his second recital, when he was lying on the hotel bed wondering what it would be like to be single again. He got his wish.

Conroy re-reads Verrier's note in hope of distraction, or perhaps because a handwritten letter – so rare a thing nowadays – is a kind of human contact we've largely forgotten. Right now, Verrier is Conroy's drinking buddy, a connoisseur, not fooled by charlatans like Paul Morrow, he can see through that sham, it was Conroy he paid to hear. The audience at Tune Inn: a few dozen too slow to make it to Morrow's sell-out. The kind of man she'd probably prefer to be sleeping with, maybe is.

Art is human, it's flawed. We make mistakes, hit wrong notes, and those great composers, they were human too, they wrote wrong notes, performers learn and repeat them. But there has to be the illusion of perfection, gleaming image of mass production and infinite reproducibility. His students at the college, he's meant to get them to competition standard, meaning they should play like machines, he shows up at work next day having slept for two hours and he's got to give lessons as usual, though all he wants is to tell them to go to hell.

When he gets a call on his office line he assumes it's Laura, grabs the receiver, skull throbbing, but it's Verrier. "Did you get the score?"

"I haven't had time to play it." Conroy's hung-over, they aren't buddies now, Verrier's unwelcome urgency has too much salesmanship about it.

"I look forward to hearing your opinion."

"I'll let you know."

Student he sees later in the week, kid called Harry, he could be the next Paul Morrow, the hair and attitude are spot-on and who gives a damn about expression? They're doing Chopin *Études*; Harry attacks the 'Winter Wind' like he's a psycho with a hunting knife, sawing his way through the right-hand sextuplets. This is competition style, all right. The two of them discuss interpretation and Harry uses the term "take-home message". What else do you expect from a generation taught to equate education with financial investment and personal debt? Conroy nods off in the middle of the next piece but is woken by a fortissimo fit for the Wembley Arena.

"How was it?" Harry asks at the end, a puppy wanting a

pat on the head.

"You've clearly been practising." This is what every teacher at every level says to every student who's just dished up for them a plateful of musical vomit.

"Thanks."

Four days of a life without Laura that began years ago, her number comes up as not recognised, she's ditched her mobile as well as her man, both equally outmoded. After Harry, Conroy has some free time and starts playing through the Klauer. This, too, he thinks, is a kind of farewell gesture, and like every artwork it's a one-way message. Klauer bowed out and left no room for a response; all we've got is a half-empty wardrobe.

Klauer's a chameleon, the first movement gives nothing away, there are possible references or allusions, but no sense of who exactly he was, this mysterious fellow with his secret knowledge. Nor did Conroy ever really know Laura; it's only when they surprise you that you find out your ignorance. We expect continuity, not paradox.

The slow movement strikes him as more readily grasped, something operatic about it, though gradually Conroy understands what the peculiar scoring and implied colours really mean. This is an idea for a symphony; these are meant to be violins, horns, an oboe. The entire work is a skeleton, and it's with this in mind that he repeats the movement, trying to guess which solo instrument is intended to be heard at the outset. In his mind a park, people in old-fashioned costume. A dull pop somewhere and a man falls to the ground. That's all there is to it, the gap between life and death.

In the afternoon he has a new student to see, a late starter on the course, must have transferred from somewhere else. When he arrives at the room she's already waiting for him, small girl, sweet smile but can't have much strength in those limbs. She says she's called Paige. He opens the sound-proof door, gestures her inside and asks, "How long have you been playing?"

"I started when I was four."

"How long is that?"

"Sixteen years."

She tells him a familiar story of lessons and grade exams, junior competitions and medals, a childhood dominated by a single lustrous project. Conroy always likes to know from the start what sort of influence the parents have had, he's seen plenty of students glad to have escaped domestic domination and wanting to take it easy. But this girl seems motivated, managed to do well in her school subjects, had other options and chose music against her parents' advice.

She offers him the *Barcarolle*, accomplished if a little stiff. Conroy finds himself trying to guess which edition she's used: Chopin wrote two slightly different manuscript versions. A left-hand D sharp soon gives it away, he stops her not long after. Next it's Beethoven, this sounds more promising, but while she plays and Conroy stares through the window at the trees and small park where a woman pushes a buggy he finds his mind drifting, the 'Waldstein' isn't holding his attention. What did Adorno say it made him think of when he was a child? Knights in a forest. Conroy must still have the book, unless Laura took it, though she seems to have been meticulously selective, removing only what was unambiguously hers. Surprising, in the Venn diagram of their material possessions, how negligible the overlap.

In Paige's performances Conroy detects a troubling in-sincerity, a desire to please out of a sense of duty. "Play me something you love," he tells her, and she offers Janacek's suite

On An Overgrown Path. An intriguing choice; its demands are expressive rather than technical. Here, thinks Conroy, is someone genuinely more interested in art than showing off. The tone feels exactly right, her playing is sensitive but restrained, completely devoid of sentimentality. She conveys what for Conroy is the real essence of this piece: the loneliness of a bad relationship. She can't possibly understand at her age, perhaps even Janacek didn't know it when he wrote the music (though he would come to know it), but Conroy can hear it as he looks down on the muted street. Truth is not something we discover consciously; it discovers us.

He turns to watch, his view of her is from the side, her concentration appears total. She looks younger than twenty. If he'd ever had a child, he thinks, he would have wanted one like this. But it's too late. It almost feels as if his life is already over.

Towards the end of the piece there's a section marked 'adagio dolcissimo'; a mysterious, floating passage that sounds like a memory, but a memory of what? If the whole piece is really about loneliness then this section is the dream of how things might otherwise have been, a false memory of happiness, a path denied. Yet this girl has so many possibilities in front of her, such potential – he hears it now – what can she know of suffering and disappointment? It moves him that she should be able to express so clearly a pain still to be felt. And this, he realises, must be the key to Pierre Klauer's music. A life full of promise, haunted by its own doomed future.

He wonders about the other path she might have taken; after she's finished he asks her what degree subject she gave up. Physics, she tells him. He's surprised, and thinks of the gauche student at his recital recently, the one who said we're all inside a box. What he meant is that we're dead in our graves from the very first moment of existence; it just takes a while to figure it out. Yes, he's sure she said physics.

Conroy decides they should spend more time on the 'Waldstein' Sonata, he understands now that all the faults he heard before were those of her teachers, she needs to unlearn what was drilled into her. He sits at the neighbouring keyboard, demonstrating passages he wants her to try, pointing out where she was apt to shorten a note, blur a chord or misplace an emphasis. In every case she takes his suggestion and turns it into something new, never mimicking, always pushing herself to experiment. So many ways to play the same piece and none is definitive, there's always room for variation. But Conroy's job is to bring her to competition standard, he's a quality-control inspector on a production line in an industry that demands consistency and predictability. He wonders if she's just too good for the professional circuit, the world of crowd-pleasing monstrosities like Tune Inn with their banal maxim of inclusivity. Paige, he senses, is an individual, not an acrobat. Beethoven is what they ought to work on but Conroy wants to hear more of that depth of feeling Paige found in the Janacek; they should go off the familiar track.

He shows her the Klauer slow movement. She takes a moment to prepare then picks up the bare opening theme, more slowly than Conroy had played it, and as the full chords enter he senses a different orchestration from what he had previously imagined. Paige's tone is warmer, the view less tragic. He can see the Paris park again, the strollers in their antiquated clothes, but now the same scene is reinterpreted and crucially altered: Klauer is a man filled with hope and optimism. Yet still he puts a gun to his head. Contradiction is the key.

"Stop there," he tells her. "When do you think it was

written?"

"Nineteen sixties?"

Conroy's first impression had been that it was typical of its era; Paige sees it as a work ahead of its time. A further reconfiguration occurs in Conroy's mind: it is not he who debuts the work, but Paige. He sets the slow movement as homework and keeps the remaining pages for himself. For the rest of the day he can't stop thinking about her, this soft-spoken brown-haired girl.

At home with a new bottle of malt whisky to console him, he studies his bookshelf, finds the work by Theodor Adorno he had thought of, opens it and sees on the yellowed front page his own signature, twice as old as the venerable drink in his glass. He looks up the story he told Paige, about the 'Waldstein', flicks and finds it, and it occurs to him: this is what the rest of your life will be like until you die. An index of former experience.

He plays through the rest of the Klauer. It isn't a lost masterpiece, such things don't exist except in minds conditioned by the preformed categories of convention, where everything possesses a measure of greatness as inherent and inviolable as the weight of a stone. To be a masterpiece means to be perceived as one; the work that is lost is unperceived, when found it is open to any kind of perception. The music speaks to Conroy of the certainty of failure, not a take-home message the public would want to hear. It says, we are all fools.

When Verrier calls a few days later, Conroy tells him at once, "I've played it."

"Splendid, I'm wondering if we could meet." He's in Conroy's town on business; perhaps they could have lunch together? Conroy suggests a place; central, bright, reasonably priced, they fix a time. Conroy arrives early, can't see anyone resembling his memory of Verrier, orders a mineral water and looks at the menu, nothing's changed since he was here before, still as false. Eventually he hears a voice, looks up, Verrier in tweed jacket is standing with an old-fashioned brown briefcase hanging from one arm, like a doctor's bag, and is extending the other across the table in greeting. He looks older than Conroy remembered, more confident now they're meeting as equals. Verrier sits and after exchanging pleasantries Conroy asks, "What's your business?"

"Property. Music's a hobby, an expensive one."

"Not if you can buy a life's work for a few quid." He's thinking of Edith Sampson's trunk.

"Sometimes you find a bargain."

The waitress comes and takes their orders, after which Verrier asks Conroy about his forthcoming concerts, the assumption being that they already exist. Conroy evasively speaks of projects he's considering, then says, "What do you think of Paul Morrow?"

"I heard his Rachmaninov recording. Do you know him?"

Conroy nods but says they're not close, he invites Verrier to be completely honest.

"Then I'd say he's still a bit raw but could well be a genius."

"A genius or a fraud?"

Verrier smiles. "Excellent question. You're not a business-man, are you? If you were, you'd appreciate how fine the dividing line can be."

"Art and business don't mix."

"But everyone has to earn a living. And if art doesn't pay, what then?"

"You mean we should all sell out, like Morrow?"

"Not his fault if he looks like a pop star. Got to make the most of the hand you're dealt."

The gambling metaphor is almost enough to put Conroy off the food that arrives soon afterwards. The waitress swiftly deposits their meals, asks automatically if they require anything else, and leaves with a swing of her hip.

"Well then, you like *The Secret Knowledge*?" Verrier enquires, bringing their meeting to its point.

"I asked one of my students when she thought it was composed..." Conroy sees a change in Verrier's expression and realises he's made an error of judgment, the work was given to him in confidence. "I showed her part of the slow movement."

"And what did she think?" Verrier asks cautiously.

"She reckoned nineteen sixties."

Now he looks indignant. "The paper and ink have been checked..."

"Of course, I'm not doubting the authenticity. And it was a stupid comment, really. But I know what she's getting at. Klauer's style is unusual, hard to pin down, not ahead of its time but outside it."

"Is it a piece you'd want to perform publicly?"

"Yes," Conroy says at once, pauses, then adds, "It'd require a lot of preparation."

"Would you have any particular venue in mind?"

Verrier is speaking like a true entrepreneur, but once more the faltering state of Conroy's career risks exposure. "Somewhere small and intimate would be best."

"Yet it seems so grand. The first movement's huge."

"Not the last, though."

Verrier nods. "I noticed that, a curious falling off. I even wondered if it might be unfinished."

The possibility occurred to Conroy when he played it; the finale opens with a melody that could be the near relation of a popular song, the movement as a whole has an atmosphere of lightness bordering on triviality. "Think of Schubert," he says. "The G major or D major sonatas, those final movements that don't go at all the way we expect, none of that Beethovenian climax and culmination. Instead something far closer to life." Klauer's finale, Conroy explains, is a *danse macabre*, a black comedy. "That's his point: things end badly."

"A marvellous theory," Verrier concedes. "And that gunshot in the park – what a superb joke!" He pushes his half-eaten salad aside and reaches down to the briefcase beside him, opening it to retrieve some pages, one of which he slides across the table to Conroy who brings his reading glasses from his pocket.

"This is the newspaper report I mentioned in my letter," Verrier explains while Conroy's eyes focus on small old print he supposes to have come from a web archive: French text announcing the tragic accident. Then a second sheet pushed beneath his view, another press extract, this time in English. Verrier points to the date in the corner, 1919, and a headline further down the page: "Agitation at public meeting." Conroy scans it without comprehension; Verrier's finger offers further assistance.

A Frenchman, M. Pierre Klauer, also took the floor, making inflammatory remarks about his countryman, the infamous revolutionary, Blanqui.

Verrier sits back with an air of triumph. "He dies in 1913 then reappears six years later."

"A different man, his namesake."

"What are the odds? Individually, the first and second names are common enough, not in combination."

"Then he didn't die? Or someone stole his identity?"

Verrier shrugs. "It's a mystery, the secret of Pierre Klauer."

"Genius or fraud," Conroy says thoughtfully.

"Possibly both. We really should try to get to the bottom of this before you premiere the work."

"None of it affects the quality of the music."

Verrier laughs. "You think so? What about the finale with its black comedy; the last word from a condemned man, or a prankster's up-yours? When Klauer wrote it, did he know he was going to fake his death and leave the country, was he already the political revolutionary he apparently turned into? Is that the secret knowledge? But leave it to me, David, I'll do the digging, you study the music. Quite a find, eh?" Verrier looks at his watch and says he has to leave for another meeting, he insists on paying, the amount too negligible to merit discussion or gratitude. The newspaper items go back inside his briefcase, his closing handshake accompanied by a voice lowered in seriousness. "I trust you not to mention this to anyone else. As owner of the manuscript, I have to ask you to keep the information confidential and your copy secure." Then he exits, leaving Conroy to ponder the enigma of Pierre Klauer, and the pages he gave his student. He phones her at once.

"Paige, it's David Conroy. There's something we need to discuss. Could we meet?"

1919

It's the evening of the meeting and the hall is full. On the platform, behind a long table, sit the committee whose nomenclature has, as Joe Baxter promised, gone unremarked, since the men and women crowding every available chair have more important concerns than spelling. John Quinn and Pierre Klauer sit side by side, Quinn rustling and reordering his scribbled notes while Klauer looks at the audience in front of him, the ranks of faces tired, determined, hopeful. He sees Jessie sitting near the front.

Quinn calls the meeting to order, his voice unsteady. He has never addressed a gathering as large as this, never seen so many hostile eyes. He quickly hands over to the regional head of one of the mining unions who outlines the case for reform, a man past fifty but still strong in appearance, his arguments clear, precise, and no different from what Quinn has been saying in print. Next is a representative of the Clyde Workers Committee who insists the campaign is not about undermining the existing order, only an attempt to create fairer working conditions and stave off the threat of mass unemployment. During the previous years there has been a working week of fifty-four hours or more, made necessary by warfare's insatiable appetite, and some groups have profited from it: the manufacturers, landlords, speculators. But war has also raised the consciousness of the workers, not afraid to strike even when the government, under the false pretence of patriotism and national unity, made striking illegal. So we must again defend ourselves, the speaker says. We must look after our own folk.

Then Pierre Klauer gets to his feet. He has no script, no notes, and for a moment appears unsure what to say, though there is no trace of nervousness or reluctance in his manner, only a calm indifference to his surroundings, as if speaking to two or three people instead of as many hundred.

"I work at the Russell factory, like many of you. And you can tell that I am a Frenchman. So I cannot say much about the history of your country but instead will say something about my own. Half a century ago, the Prussians reached the outskirts of Paris and laid siege. The people ran out of meat and had to kill dogs and cats and horses. Zoo elephants were slaughtered and served to restaurant diners. The poor ate rats, until even the rats were gone. The government in Versailles capitulated, but not the people of Paris. Governments are often less patriotic than those they claim to represent. So while it suited Thiers and his cronies to make peace with German industrialists, the workers thought otherwise, and declared Paris a socialist republic, a commune that would fight on.

"The communards imprisoned various members of the ruling class; Thiers demanded their release. And the communards told him, we will free everyone if you in turn release, out of all the many political prisoners you hold, just one, the man we have chosen to be our president. Thiers said no. He signed a humiliating peace treaty with Prussia, and the commune was suppressed. Thousands of innocent men, women and children were slaughtered; shot or bayoneted as they tried to flee, lined against walls in summary executions until the streets of Paris were washed with proletarian blood.

"Who was the man Thiers feared so much that he would allow the deaths of all these people, and the hostages too, rather than free him to join the insurrection? His name was Louis-Auguste Blanqui. He had wielded a musket when Charles the Tenth was overthrown, was on the streets in 1848, and had suffered for it, kept in solitary confinement at Mont Saint-Michel in conditions that would have driven many men insane. At Belle Ile he grew so sick he was released in order to die – but instead this man with an iron constitution recovered and continued the struggle, until the grimy Fortress of Taureau became his final home.

"Blanqui was a small, wiry man, not at all handsome, prematurely aged by incarceration, white-haired by his forties, his face hollow, his clothes shabby. One day when he was in prison they told him his wife had died; he had barely seen her, or their son. He gave his life to the cause of revolution, renounced all human pleasure, all comfort, expected nothing except hardship. To someone like Thiers, feasting in Versailles with German bankers while the whole of Paris starved, this was incomprehensible. How can any man value justice more than money? How can anyone love freedom so much that he is prepared to spend three-quarters of his life in prison? You see, my friends, to the capitalist mentality, self-sacrifice is a mystery greater than the transubstantiation of the Host. A man who will not give a coin to a beggar will never understand someone willing to give his life for a stranger he calls comrade."

John Quinn isn't watching the speaker beside him, only the audience, puzzled at first, but gradually warming to Klauer's theme of brotherhood. The Frenchman quotes Robert Burns, hums Beethoven's 'Ode To Joy', cracks a joke that raises a laugh. Men and women gaze with growing admiration, charmed by Klauer's foreign manner, flattered by his praise of their country's liberal traditions, stirred by vivid tales of struggle.

"So you see, my friends, if justice is on our side then it doesn't matter how few we might be in number, because numbers can grow. We have heard how the forty-hour week will mean there will be enough work for everyone. We have heard that the employers, too, must sacrifice a modest portion of their profits to the common good. What does this small gesture count for, against the blood of our own loved ones, spilled in the trenches? Do we not owe it to them, and to the ones who survive? Are we like the speculators of Versailles, who knew the value of nothing except money? Or are we communards, patriots, workers united?"

Applause breaks out, there are shouts as people rise to their feet.

"Workers united!"

"We'll show them!"

The plan was for questions and answers, instead there is confusion, a babble John Quinn is unable to suppress when he calls for order, and nor can the union man, who reminds everyone that the Trades Council has yet to pass a motion on the issue and action must not be taken until then. Pierre, smiling at what he has achieved, makes no effort to quieten the room where everyone has now risen; instead he goes down from the podium and joins the crowd, greeted by a few handshakes and backslaps and then by Jessie, her face illuminated with wonder, her remark to him inaudible, lost in the general mood of congratulation, so that he draws closer and asks her to say it in his ear, puts his arm round her while she tells him he was superb.

There is a loud banging from the chairman on stage, now armed with a gavel someone has rescued from a storeroom. John Quinn looks like the student he is, young and overwhelmed, yet it is his hand that holds the hammer, and the audience's reaction is instinctively deferential. They begin returning to their seats.

Pierre says softly to Jessie, "Come outside with me."

"What?"

"I need some air after the speech."

Amid the general movement of people reminded of the decorum expected of them, Pierre pushes to the exit with Jessie following behind, and they emerge onto the dark street.

"It's cold," Jessie exclaims.

"Then have my overcoat." He removes it before she can protest, and wraps it over her shoulders.

"You're very gallant. And such a good speaker. Have you done much before?"

"Not really."

"I can't believe it, you were so confident. If I'd been in front of that many people I'd have fainted."

"I know something about performance," he says.

In the poor light she looks quizzically at him, but Pierre doesn't elaborate, nor even notice her curiosity. It unsettles her. "We really oughtn't stand here."

"You're still cold?"

"It might appear odd, the two of us."

"Why odd?"

"As if we're together."

"Aren't we?"

"That's not what I mean." She gives an embarrassed laugh,

then adds seriously, "People might conclude we're a couple."

Pierre is unconcerned. "Does it matter what people conclude?"

"It would if they told my father. Not that he'd mind. But he'd want to know first."

He takes her hands in his. "Your father has been so generous and welcoming, I almost feel as if you and John were my own brother and sister. I would never wish to do anything that might be misinterpreted."

"I know."

"If we were to walk together it would only be as friends, anyone can see that. So why don't we? Better than standing here, surely."

He adjusts the large and heavy coat that hangs around her shoulders, making sure she's adequately protected, and they begin to stroll slowly as if it were an afternoon in summer, not a harsh January night. Jessie, previously so talkative, is made quieter by the new situation; instead it's Pierre who leads the conversation in the same way that he guides his companion, with a gentle insistence pushing towards some unknown but predetermined goal.

"I don't think those people really understood what I was talking about, but at least they learned something. Let's go this way."

"The river? It's so dark."

"But perfectly safe."

"I might step in a puddle."

"I'll make sure you don't." He puts his arm round her waist. "Come, your eyes will soon adjust. Let's imagine we're in Paris and the air is warmer."

She does as he says. They are in a place she knows from books and magazines, a place of dreams and romance, where it is permissible for her to lean against him until she can feel his breath on her hair. Soon they reach a bench and he suggests they sit; she expects the cold to seize her but is protected from it by his coat and his own body so close to hers, his arm around her as determined as a helmsman's. The moon appears from behind a passing cloud and she sees the gently moving water glisten in front of them.

"Are you afraid?" he asks.

"Why should I be?"

"You were before."

"I was only scared of getting wet. I know this path well enough in the daytime. That's the memorial over there." It's like a shadowed finger against the indigo sky. "I played there with John when we were wee."

"And now you're grown."

"Yes."

"I'd like to kiss you."

"No." She's said it so quickly, already she's reconsidering. "It's not right."

"Have I offended you?"

"I like you very much, Pierre. But we don't really know each other. I've never done anything like this before."

"Do you mind my having my arm around you?"

"Just don't squeeze."

"Of course."

"In Paris I suppose it's different. Did you have a sweetheart there?"

"Yes."

Her heart suddenly feels like stone. "Did you love her a great deal?"

"I wanted to marry her."

Jessie edges away but feels his arm still restraining her,

unwilling to let go.

"She was called Yvette," he explains.

"Was she pretty?"

"Like a painting. I've no idea what happened to her. My life in France is over, I have a new one now."

In Paris he adored a proud and fashionable beauty; here he is now with a plain little red-haired girl from a town no one has heard of, inviting her to join the story-book list of his conquests. She feels both elevated and crushed by Yvette's spectre floating haughtily in her mind.

"Was it because of her you left?"

"You could say so. I wanted her to be my wife but knew my father would never approve."

"You could have eloped."

Pierre laughs. "Yes, we could have. To be with Yvette I was willing to give up everything. I hadn't seen her for a few weeks but wrote and told her to meet me at a fair that was being held. I planned to propose to her as we rode together on the big wheel."

"That's so romantic."

"We met and I saw her face again after what felt like such a long time… but something had changed. I had become a new person and so, I think, had she."

"After only a few weeks of separation?"

"Much had happened. I'd begun to see that my life, in many ways, was empty and without purpose. I'd discovered a new mission, a goal, and I wanted Yvette to share it with me, but as soon as I saw her, I wondered if she was the right person."

"What mission? A religious one? I haven't noticed you in chapel…"

"I can't explain it, Jessie. I wanted to tell Yvette but never had the chance. We went on the big wheel and were whirled up into the air, it was beautiful. I asked her to marry me. She said yes."

"You must both have been so happy." Jessie feels stiff within his grip.

"We came off and toured the fair, I was jubilant but at the same time doubtful, fearful. I had a great decision to make, a terrible choice. There was not one life that lay before me but many, a junction of possibilities, a test. There was something I had to do. I told Yvette to wait for me. It was only a small piece of business I had arranged with a friend, a task of a few minutes."

"Could she not have come with you?"

"No, that was the test I put her to. A moment alone, then a lifetime together."

"Did you tell her where you were going?"

"I said I'd explain afterwards. You see what a simple thing I asked of her, this woman who not long before had agreed to love me forever! Yet she refused."

"It's not polite to make a lady wait," Jessie says.

"But this was about trust and faith. I gave her the key to my writing desk, something very precious and important to me, and insisted she stay holding it while I attended to my business."

In Paris, thinks Jessie, everything is so different; the people are like costumed actors on a stage, yet more real than anything here in Kenzie. She can see the drama of the key, can almost feel its metal as though it were she who was made to wait. Yes, she thinks, if I truly loved a man then I would wait for him not minutes, but years, an eternity.

"So I left her standing there, I remember the place so well, near a tent where an acrobat was performing. I went, and after only a short time the task was finished."

"What exactly was this business of yours?"

"I told you, Jessie, it was a test, nothing more."

"You mean you only wanted Yvette to wait? What about the mission you mentioned?"

"This was my mission, right there in the park. A new world, transformed and radiant, made pure by love and faith. I prayed, Jessie. I went to a place near the boating pond and prayed. I asked myself, what is this life? What is the future? What is our place in the universe? And it was like an earthquake in my heart. Out of so many paths, I chose the one I knew must already have been chosen for me, there could be no other, I had only to take it and see what it was like. I hurried back, ran so fast that people stared, wondering if I was mad, I expect a few thought I must be chasing a thief or was being pursued by one. I reached the spot – and she was gone. I couldn't believe it, I called out for her, and then to the gods who'd tricked me, I dropped to my knees and clawed the grass, searching for what I knew I must eventually find. And there it was, gleaming in the sunshine, the little key."

He falls silent and Jessie feels the grave-like stillness of the moonlit night, the desolation of solitude. Her dull and dirty town is reborn, crystalline, hard yet fragile as the ice in her blood. "If you wish, you may kiss me now."

His lips burn against hers. This was what Yvette refused to wait for, this new life of faith he discovered in himself, this animal breath and bitter tang of tobacco, this rub of stubble and rising excitement – his fingers searching for her.

"Stop." She pulls away.

"Forgive me."

"It's not your fault, only we don't do that here." There is a void of cold air between them. She wants him to hold her hand but is unable to reach for his. "Did you ever see her again?"

"Her message was clear. I never wrote or contacted her. My old life was finished and I had to begin a new one. So I came to Britain, then the war started."

"John told me you were interned. How sad you must have felt in prison, how desperately lonely. I imagine you thought of her every day."

"I decided not to."

"Was it really so easy?"

"No, but it was possible. I knew that whatever I did must be right, somehow. Even if it didn't appear that way at the time. Jessie, I want to kiss you again, properly."

"Not now."

"You make me so glad I lost Yvette."

She can't tell if it's blushes or tears she feels rushing to her face. "You shouldn't say that."

"But it's true. You're a sweet and beautiful girl." He reaches for her hand and she cradles his fingers on her lap.

"I would have waited."

"I'm sure you would."

"The way you told me about Yvette, and what you said at the meeting – you're so honest and open. You truly believe in people, that's what I feel. You believe in them because you believe in yourself. But you can get hurt that way, like with Yvette, aren't you worried it might happen again? With the workers' campaign, for instance. You could get into trouble for what you said."

"I don't care."

"Even if you finished up back in gaol?"

"That can't happen."

"The man you mentioned in your speech, the rebel, he spent most of his life in prison. You surely don't want that."

"Blanqui never feared the consequences of adhering to his

principles, I admire that."

"He hardly saw his wife and son, how must it have been for them?"

"You're right, it might have been kinder had he never married." He looks back along the path as if expecting to see someone, but it remains quiet. "The meeting will soon be over."

"We should return."

"Or we could walk a little further. I could even take you home."

"John will be wondering where we are. Let's go as far as the monument, then turn back."

They walk hand in hand, Jessie's fingers immobile and stiffening. Soon they reach the granite obelisk that is like a polished tomb; Pierre tries to see its inscription in the weak light. "I've passed this before but I've never read what's on it."

Jessie knows and can decipher it for him. "*On 31st December 1860, during severe flooding, James Deuchar, 20, a divinity student at Glasgow University, leapt into the river near this spot in an attempt to rescue George Laidlaw, 5, and Mary Laidlaw, 7, who had fallen in. Having saved the younger child, Mr Deuchar returned to search for the girl, who was washed up alive further downstream. Mr Deuchar, however, perished in his noble endeavour. This monument to his heroism was erected by public subscription, 3rd January 1863.*"

"Nearly sixty years ago," Pierre calculates.

"He could still have been alive, an old man now."

"Better that he died doing good. Think of all those men buried beneath the battlefields without even a wooden cross to mark them. History has become a factory, its heroes no longer have names."

"Would you like your name to go down in history, Pierre?"

"That's a foolish ambition and if Deuchar had thought that way he would never have jumped in. He cared only about saving life, even if it meant losing his own. As I said in my speech, Jessie, it's what capitalism can never explain nor comprehend. The industrialists made no sacrifice in the war, only profit, through making others sacrifice themselves."

Jessie is shivering. "Let's return."

They walk with hands pushed inside their pockets. He tells her, "After the Paris Commune fell, when Blanqui had been in solitary confinement so long he could barely speak, he wrote a remarkable book. It says the same arrangements of atoms must come up again and again throughout space, in every possible variation. There must be a planet with another you, another me."

"He was a romantic after all," says Jessie.

"On one of them right now I'm making the speech in the meeting hall. On another I'm…"

"With Yvette?"

"I suppose. Every moment is an eternity in space. Blanqui says it in his book."

"Prison drove him mad."

"It made him see circumstances differently."

"Like your earthquake in the park?"

"There are worlds where Deuchar drowned and others where he survived."

"Let's talk about something else."

"But don't you understand, Jessie? There's a world where he goes back and saves another child, and another. He walks into burning houses, collapsing buildings, and escapes without a scratch. There's a world where Deuchar knows himself to be immortal."

He seizes and kisses her.

"Stop it, Pierre."

"Don't you feel the eternity of the stars?"

It fills her body, she longs to surrender to it, but not now. She breaks away and they continue in silence to the hall, arriving there as the crowd are preparing to leave. A new world has been born inside her.

She doesn't see Pierre again until the weekend. It's Saturday afternoon and she's at the piano, hasn't played for months, the instrument's in need of tuning but she's been gripped by a renewed urge to touch those yellowed keys whose vibrations are like a secret acknowledgment of her thoughts. Father is reading, she hears the occasional turning of a page behind her, and in her mind the words of the song she plays. *You have loved lots of girls in the sweet long ago and each one has meant heaven to you.* She doesn't notice the knock at the front door; father tells her to go and see who it is. She finds Pierre waiting on the step, straight from the end of his shift, and feels herself redden. But he hasn't come for her; it's John he's looking for, there's urgency in his voice.

"Is something wrong? Come inside and tell me."

"I expected to see him at the factory. The strike's going ahead."

"At Russell?"

"Everywhere. All of Glasgow will be out on Monday." Pierre brings in cold air with him and removes his cap. "Scobie, the shop steward, told us this morning, says the union still won't back it though everyone I've spoken to is willing to walk out. Where the blazes is that brother of yours?"

It's as if none of it ever happened. She knows it has to be this way. "My father's in there, go and say hello."

Dr Quinn has heard Pierre's raised voice though not his words. "*Bonjour*, Monsieur Klauer," he says from his chair, pleasantly but with cool detachment, his professional bedside manner. "If you're looking for John I don't know where he is. You could always try again later."

"Are you hungry?" Jessie asks from behind Pierre's back. He turns. "That's very kind."

"We've eaten already," says her father. "I suppose Jessie could fetch you something."

She goes to the kitchen, Pierre waits for an invitation to sit but none comes, so he perches on the piano stool, facing away from the instrument and towards Dr Quinn who looks at his book, unable to read, then eventually says, "I hear you made a fine speech the other night."

"Thank you, sir."

"A forty-hour week. I wonder if I've ever done so few. You're all finished for the day and I'm only starting, I'll be making my rounds soon."

"I'm sure everyone appreciates what you do."

The doctor believes he detects some sarcasm. "You're sure are you? I don't think anyone appreciates the work I have to do. And this son of mine, ought to be studying but doesn't know the meaning of work." He looks penetratingly at Pierre, something on his mind he's now prepared to raise. "I asked John if he knew you from prison. He said no."

"I was at Stobs camp."

"I know that, I checked with a policeman friend of mine."

Pierre is acquainted with such frank suspicion, untroubled by it. "My name was my misfortune."

The doctor appears almost sympathetic. "Must have been hard for you, locked up with Germans. Your enemy as much as ours."

"They'd been living in this country for years."

"What about bolshevists? Were there many of them in the

camp?"

"Not really."

Dr Quinn proceeds towards his chosen point with clinical precision. "My son's no revolutionary, he's an idealist. This newspaper of his is only a game."

"You worry I'm a bad influence."

"Yes, I do. Of course any man's entitled to his opinions and I believe in free speech as much as you. But where can a man speak freely if not in his own home? So I tell you honestly, Pierre, while I respect the strength of your convictions, even feel a degree of sympathy for them, I fear the possible consequences. Just look at what happened in Russia, and now in Germany, uprisings all over the place, bringing nothing but sorrow. Maybe you want to become a martyr like that confounded Luxemburg woman, that's your choice, but my son didn't survive four years of war in order to get himself shot on a barricade."

He stops when he sees Jessie enter. She's fried some bacon, the smell comes with her. "Shall I bring it here?" she asks father, who shows no sign of anger in the wake of his outburst, able to retain objectivity even when contemplating tragedy. He calmly sends both of them to the kitchen so that he can read. Pierre sits down there and begins to eat, chewing thoughtfully while Jessie stands watching in silence. She heard none of the conversation but perceived its tension. Eventually she tells him, almost whispering, "I haven't said anything about our walk."

Pierre looks up at her, somehow puzzled that she should mention it. "Probably best," he agrees.

She sits down too, lays her hand on the table, outstretched fingers not far from his resting elbow, and waits for him to say something more, though all he can do is cut crisp shreds of meat, transporting them mechanically to his mouth.

"Do you think I should tell father?"

"He wouldn't approve."

"Then what do we do?" It's a great problem to which she has given much thought. Pierre asks her to pour him some tea. She says with hardly suppressed anguish, "Must we stop going together?"

"What do you prefer?"

"I don't know."

Pierre can't see what's so complicated; the world is about to be reborn and this girl worries over a triviality. "I think we should carry on in secret."

"You do?"

"It's not as if we're doing anything wrong."

"But we… you know." Gripped by romantic horror she feels the magnetic force of his body just beyond her fingertips, remembers his kiss.

He smiles. "We can do it again. Nobody need know."

"I'm not like that."

From the other room her father calls; she goes to be told that if Pierre has been served she should carry on playing the piano as before, Dr Quinn finds it soothing, their guest will too. At the first chords, Pierre comes and stands in the doorway, watching with folded arms.

"Sit and listen," the doctor instructs him.

It's a music-hall song neither man recalls, but the words are in Jessie's thoughts as she plays. *I wonder who's kissing her now, wonder who's teaching her how. Wonder who's looking into her eyes, breathing sighs, telling lies.* A postcard that was on the sheet music when she lifted it has a soldier standing guard at the front while in the corner, like a floating angel, a beautiful woman clutches a rose to her bosom, waiting faithfully for her lover to return. Yvette must have looked like that, she thinks.

"Do you play an instrument?" Dr Quinn asks Klauer.

"None at all."

"But you like music, you told me."

"Only listening."

"Jessie has a fine touch, such an expressive legato."

"I'm no expert."

She suddenly stops and turns. "I've had enough."

"We were enjoying it," her father says.

"My hands are tired. I want to go for a walk. Pierre, would you like to come with me?" Both men are surprised by the proposal. "You're starting your rounds soon, father, it would be rude to leave Pierre waiting here on his own."

Dr Quinn can see the logic; it's a polite way of getting the Frenchman out of the house. "You two go for some air, then. But not far, your brother should be back soon and he'll be needing fed." He doesn't see the glance that passes between the young pair as Jessie goes to fetch her coat and hat.

Outside it's grey and damp but she's glad to have him by her side, her French beau, almost wants him to put his arm round her, though instead he keeps a polite distance between them, saying nothing. She can tell he's thinking about the strike, walking more swiftly than she'd prefer, almost as if wanting to get away from her. She can't see the point of the dispute, nor understand how the men can possibly get what they want; it's a battle over an impossible dream. Only when Pierre spoke at the meeting did she feel persuaded by the argument.

He pauses, turns. "There's something I have to ask of you." His hesitancy ominously magnifies the possibilities.

"Anything."

"The union's against us."

"I know that."

"They've declared there's to be no strike pay." His fingers play nervously together in fumbled prayer. "Already I'm behind with bills…"

"I can help you."

"I wouldn't dream of it!"

"Then what?"

"Your father; I'm sure he must have some cash around the house that he'd never miss."

She's shocked, horrified by the mere suggestion, yet brings it to its conclusion. "Yes."

"I'd soon repay it."

"I trust you."

"If your father found out…"

"He won't, he never looks."

"The last thing I'd want would be to get you into trouble."

He should take her in his arms right now, here in the street, she wouldn't resist. He should kiss her in view of anyone who might pass. "Tell me how much you need."

His expression changes. "How much could you get?"

Now they're negotiating, they've crossed a boundary; Jessie, darkly thrilled by the moral calculus, considers her own wage when she was packing shells at Russell. "Would fifteen shillings do?" Pierre hesitates to answer; she says, "More?"

"I'm in arrears, even two or three pounds wouldn't be enough, and if the strike continues…"

"I'll find whatever I can." The bargain is closed by a clasping together of their hands.

Pierre smiles. "One day, when times are better, I'll be able to reward you properly."

She repeats softly, "One day." The future is feathered, comforting, just beyond reach; a marriage bed.

"Shall I walk you home again?"

"Father will have left, if we don't go too quickly."

"And then?"

Then anything: love, dreams, revolution, she wants the future right now. "I'll give you the money."

Their pace is as measured and deliberate as the ticking of a clock. He's asking her to do something bold and courageous but his own risk is surely greater. There'll be picketing, he tells her, the police will doubtless intervene and a few heads may be split.

"You have to be careful." She never had a gallant soldier to pray for, not even her brother.

"I know how to take care of myself."

Nearing the house, she tells him to wait while she goes ahead to check. If the place is empty she will draw a curtain as signal that he should come and knock. It's like something from one of those French novels she's secretly read; life transfigured by a higher honesty known only to the heart. God will forgive all this – as long as father never knows.

Pierre Klauer stands as instructed until at a window he sees the movement that equals her surrender. To visit a woman and be paid for it: that's new. The door opens for him without anyone visible beyond; when she closes it he immediately goes to kiss her.

"No."

"But we're alone."

"We have to be careful. John might be back any minute."

Bolt the door and leave the fool standing outside, Klauer thinks; leave him waiting until they're finished and getting dressed again. He takes her in his arms, his immortal arms, and tastes the sweetness of her lips.

She pulls away with some reluctance. "I'll fetch that

money."

Still in his coat he goes to the sitting room, looks at the piano and the song sheet open on it, feels a deep urge to sit and make generous music, while from the kitchen comes the rattle of china, a lid being lifted and a jar replaced. His life is like the flicking of a false coin. She comes to the kitchen doorway and stands with the gift in her hands, a bouquet of crumpled notes.

"Four pounds," she says.

"He stores so much for housekeeping?"

"It's not that."

"Then what?" He goes to her, cups his hands round the warmth of hers.

"I saved this from when I was working."

"You'll have it all back soon." He puts the crisp bundle into his pocket without looking at it, both of them ashamed by its presence. Then he holds her waist and she lets him kiss her more fully, she folds into him likc a vine, he pecks at her ear and she gasps with surprise and uncertainty.

"I love you," he says.

She knows what happens next in those French novels, but could she really do it, make herself into an Yvette? She wishes a great cannon were about to destroy everything, then she'd have the courage; only death can equal the magnitude of what she feels.

"John will be back."

"I don't care."

"Father might have forgotten something."

"If anyone calls we ignore it or escape through the back door."

She laughs. "You're a monster!"

"I'm in love with you, that's all. When you're in love nothing is forbidden, everything is allowed." There's solemnity in his voice.

"Everything?" she repeats.

"The whole world. The universe." He releases her. "Look at this." When he reaches into his coat she expects him to take out a little box with a ring inside, a fantasy replaced just as quickly by another, a photograph of the woman Jessie has supplanted, Yvette in Parisian finery. Yet neither emerges; what he instead produces is something it takes a moment for her to recognise and comprehend, black and terrible in his hand. He holds it by its muzzle, a small pistol.

"By the good Lord, why do you have such a thing?"

He displays it with boastful pride. "Just in case."

"But it's dangerous, unlawful. You have to be rid of it."

"It's harmless, there's no bullet." He puts it to the side of his head and pulls the trigger, she screams as the little weapon gives a click, hears her own scream reverberate, gasps and bursts into tears.

"Don't cry, silly woman."

His arms try to encircle her again, but at the end of one of them is the gun she feels pressing on her. "Why show me that horrible thing?" she sobs. "You're not going to take it to the picket are you? Pierre, you're frightening me."

"Calm yourself." He puts it back inside his coat and wipes her cheek with his finger. "There are no rules except whatever we make for ourselves. I love you, Jessie." The words sound different now. "I want to know how much you love me."

"Can't you tell already?" A sound startles her, someone trying the front door. "It's John."

"Does he have a key?"

"He's always forgetting it."

Pierre grabs her waist again, one-handed, a gesture filled with bravado. "Let him find his key, then."

She goes past him to answer the door, hurriedly drying her eyes. "We'll say you just arrived."

"It's the truth."

Klauer hears him enter, Jessie rapidly explaining to him the situation, but as soon as John comes into the sitting room there are other matters to discuss.

"So the strike's definite?"

"I expect at least a hundred of us at the picket line, John. But we need more."

"From the works?"

"Anywhere, it's a general stoppage." Pierre claps his friend's shoulder as if trying to rouse him from sleep. "This is what you've been wanting, isn't it?"

John's dazed expression is not because of the strike; he's wondering exactly how long Pierre has been here, what the two of them have been saying about him. He sits to collect his thoughts.

"If it's a hundred on the first day it'll be everyone on the second," Pierre tells him. "By the end of the week the whole country will be in the grip of the workers. This is the moment of revolution."

A frown crosses John's childlike face. "This is about jobs for heroes, not revolt."

"Call it whatever you wish," says Pierre. "It's out of our hands now, you can't stop history. You're not scared, are you?"

John shoots him an angry look. "Of course not."

Jessie goes to her brother. "If there's any sign of trouble, John, you keep clear of it, do you hear me?"

"Oh, there'll be trouble," Pierre assures her.

"Then leave John out of this. He has nothing to do with Russell, why should he picket?"

Both of them are talking over his head, John says nothing,

until finally Pierre stares down at him. "Your father's right, this is only a game to you."

"Go to hell."

In an instant the scene erupts; Pierre has grasped the other man round the neck, locking him where he sits, Jessie screams but her voice becomes strangled by terror, the gun has been pulled out and is held against John's head, he pants with fear. Jessie manages to speak through the pain she feels. "It's not loaded, John, he doesn't mean it, for the love of God, Pierre, stop this madness."

Pierre's eyes are like lead. "It's loaded, Jessie."

"Have mercy!" John pleads, and at last Pierre frees him, slumped and weeping in his sister's arms. Looking proudly at them both, Pierre raises the gun to his own head and defiantly squeezes the trigger, creating nothing but a snap of metal, a brief interruption to the others' anguished moans. Then without a word he leaves them both.

It is some hours later when there is a knock at the door; Jessie's eyes are still red from crying and she takes a moment to arrange herself in front of the mirror before opening, expecting a request for the doctor who is nevertheless still out. Instead it's a policeman and a large, grim-faced man she recognises, Mr Scobie from the Russell factory. They tell her they've come about Klauer.

"A friend of the family, I understand," the constable says, coming inside.

"Not any more."

The men exchange a glance; John comes to see what's amiss.

"I knew from the outset he was no good," says Scobie. "This latest only confirms it. He's been passing himself off with forged papers."

"What do you mean?" Jessie asks.

The policeman explains. "I've checked the records and can't find a trace of him anywhere. The man's an impostor, a fraud. Whoever the devil he is, you can be sure he's not Pierre Klauer."

Chapter Four

In face of the dictatorship of banality the choice becomes inescapable between conformism or resistance. Conroy is at home practising *The Secret Knowledge* when it occurs to him that he forgot to ask Paige what she thinks of that dickhead charlatan Paul Morrow.

Klauer's music encapsulates the fraught opposition between autonomy and commodification that is the essence of bourgeois art. Already while Conroy plays, the programme note is writing itself inside his head, he can almost hear the flutter of its page from a distracted audience member at the concert premiere. What the crowd comes to worship is not music, but the money spent on admission. Hard to sustain a performing career with that sort of attitude, though. Conroy takes a break.

He tries to remember what exactly was Adorno's phrase; not dictatorship of banality, he thinks, but banality of perfection, the demand that every musician become the flawless imitation of a recording. He's about to go and look it up when he hears the doorbell, goes to answer and sees what appears to be a tradesman soliciting work. Strongly-built, closely cropped reddish-brown hair, casually dressed in a zippered black leather jacket and holding up some kind of identity card. It's only when Conroy hears the word "police" that the interruption to his day makes sense. "You came about Laura?"

"Mind if I step inside?"

Conroy takes the plainclothes officer to the music room and invites him to sit on the couch. The policeman – Conroy didn't catch his name – looks admiringly at the grand piano.

"You're a teacher?"

"Concert performer. I also do some college teaching."

Inspector something, Conroy thinks, this is what he mentally calls the tall man looking hunched and slightly crumpled on the sofa that seems rather too small for him. Conroy wonders if he should offer the inspector some tea but senses the need to go straight to the issue. "She simply vanished, took away everything that's hers. I said it all on the phone, don't know how much they told you…"

The police officer makes a cordial but dismissive gesture that silences Conroy. "I'm here about something else. There was some suspicious activity in the street last night. A resident saw two youths loitering, thought they might be trying to break into a house. She phoned and a patrol car came round but they'd gone. Turns out a gentleman at the end of the street has had his car vandalised. Did you hear any disturbance last night? See anything unusual? Lady reckons it must have been around one o'clock in the morning."

Conroy would have been awake but remembers nothing, he'd had too much whisky by then. "I called yesterday about my partner Laura."

"I know."

"Shouldn't we be discussing that?"

"It's not really a police matter."

"But she's disappeared completely, took everything. Clothes, books, photos…"

"Then it was her own choice."

"Her phone number's no longer recognised. And strangest of all is the internet, not a sign of her. She's a freelance journalist, it shouldn't be hard to find someone like that, even if she's closed down her online accounts."

The officer looks penetratingly at Conroy. "Has it occurred to you that she might have decided to take anti-stalking measures?"

Conroy's stunned. "I'm not a stalker, I'm her partner."

"Not any more."

"But how could she erase herself so quickly? Surely she'd need help…" Then, seeing the officer's impassive expression, Conroy asks incredulously, "Would the police be involved in that?"

"Might be," the officer says. "Though you can see that I wouldn't be able to comment on it. I honestly don't know what's gone on in this instance, but it seems your ex has taken extreme steps to tell you it's finished and you shouldn't try finding her. Best leave it at that." His eyes show a glimmer of pity. "Always hard when things break down. Just have to move on." He gets to his feet, Conroy thinks he's about to leave, but instead the policeman walks over to the grand piano and looks at the pages of the Klauer score. "My wife plays a bit. Nothing like this I expect. Doesn't mean a thing to me, might as well be some sort of secret formula. You practise a lot?"

"Every day," Conroy says to the back of his head, while the officer continues his dumb admiration of the musical notation until the fingers of his left hand idly move down to the keys and strike a random discord, clumsy and intrusive. Conroy wants him to go now but the inspector still hasn't finished, he turns to look at framed photographs on the wall.

"This you, Mr Conroy?"

"I won a prize."

"You seem very young."

"It was a long time ago." Better take down those old pictures, Conroy thinks. Burn them all. Move on.

"And you're sure you didn't hear anything at all last night?"

"I must have been asleep."

"Lady who phoned, I don't want to worry you, she said she thought they were lurking round your house. I had a look at your front door before I came in and couldn't see anything untoward, but I think we should perhaps check in case there's been any attempted entry." The officer goes to the window, peers around the frame, then comes back past Conroy who follows him into the kitchen where the policeman makes the same quick assessment. It seems he wants to view the whole house, even asking if he might look upstairs. Conroy assents with a shrug and leaves him to get on with it, choosing to return to the music room where he sits on the piano stool hearing creaks and footsteps above as the survey continues.

After a few minutes the officer comes back to join him. "All looks fine," he says, returning to his place on the sofa, still not ready to leave. "Certainly no indication that anyone might have tried breaking in."

"I would have heard if they did."

"Not necessarily. Did you have any visitors last night?"

"No."

"The youths the lady saw might have come out of your house. She could have got the wrong idea."

"I didn't have any visitors."

"Can you remind me roughly what time you phoned yesterday about your partner?"

"Early evening."

It was after Conroy got back from college, he listened to some music, had a drink, went on the internet and did what he'd been resisting, he searched for Laura, even if it was only to see her face again. But she wasn't there, he panicked, and at some point decided to phone the police, though he couldn't recall exactly when, or what he might have said.

The officer makes a suggestion. "Six or seven o'clock, perhaps?"

"Probably later."

"Before nine? I can check, of course."

"You'd better do that. I was busy, I easily lose track of time."

"We all know the feeling," the policeman says with a smile that soon fades. "I couldn't help noticing the empty bottles in the kitchen. I know this must be a rough time for you. What I'm saying is that if you need some kind of help…"

"I don't need that kind."

"People phone the police for all sorts of reasons."

"It seemed sinister, like she'd been rubbed out."

"And now? Doesn't look that way, does it? Only reason I came here is because of those youths seen hanging about, and I'm quite prepared to believe there's an innocent explanation for that too. Can you remember what time you made your second call last night?"

"Second?"

"You phoned twice. I haven't seen the record but from what I hear, you were a bit lippy next time round." Waiting for a response that Conroy is unable to make, the officer has the emotionless face of someone who has seen every kind of human distress, someone for whom this is the smallest of routine occurrences. "People often get impatient, it's natural.

They think there's an emergency and they want sirens to come blazing round the corner as soon as they've put the phone down. You've done nothing wrong, Mr Conroy, you're in a bad place at the moment, I know it must be hard."

"I called only once."

The policeman shakes his head. "We can all be forgetful after a drink or two. Especially if we're not having the best of times. And your private life is no business of mine, but if you think you know who those two lads could have been you might as well tell me. As far as I can see this whole thing's about nothing more than a snapped wing mirror, possibly not even that."

"I had no visitors."

He stands up. "That's all, then, Mr Conroy. Thanks for your time. You won't phone again about your ex, will you? And I really don't think you should try finding her. Do what you want on the internet but don't take it any further. Otherwise you could wind up with a court order and you wouldn't want that."

Conroy stares in helpless fury and humiliation. "You think I'm dangerous? Violent?"

"Your second call last night was well out of order and I don't want it happening again. I know it was the drink talking but we don't stand for that sort of behaviour. Take my advice, get some help if you need it, move on with your life." He glances at the piano again. "Don't let your talent go to waste." Then he makes his way out, followed by Conroy who closes the door on him with a sense of disbelief.

There was no second call, the idiot got his facts wrong and only need check the record. Conroy's tempted to phone and complain but it might simply encourage further harassment. Instead he goes back to the piano to resume playing and attacks the keyboard with full strength. Anger gives a satisfying edge to his fortissimo. How could anyone possibly think he would stalk her? He wanted it to end, his secret death-wish for a relationship that had long been in a state of half-life.

In everything there is a latent inconsistency awaiting realisation. Klauer's music: beautiful and hideous. Laura: generous and cruel. Story she was chasing about a big multinational, something like that. His fingers stumble, he stops playing then repeats the problem passage. He should take it all more carefully, do what he tells his own students, never try to cover up technical weakness but instead work to find the source of the problem then eliminate it. So many hidden cracks.

Genius or fraud, the programme note might pose the question regarding Klauer but could equally apply to Conroy himself. When he told the policeman he was a concert performer he could feel his throat tightening; a description of what he once was, nowadays he's not sure. In a world as sick as ours only liars and cheats can profit, commodified con-artists like Morrow. He'll go back to the difficult passage later, meanwhile he carries on with the movement, bringing himself back to speed and wondering why the policeman needed to take so long to give him a ticking off over a pissed phone call.

And suddenly it hits him. The policeman was a fake. He leaps up from the piano stool as if struck by an electric shock. That man, whoever he was, wandered round the house unattended, he could have helped himself to anything. Conroy runs upstairs and inspects each room, looking in drawers, checking on items of value. He never leaves money lying around, the only jewellery was Laura's, but in the bedroom he conducts a meticulous search for his own property and any sign of intrusion. He has nothing worth stealing, nothing the man could have hidden inside his zippered jacket, but the thought nags him that he may have been duped. The clock on the bedside table, has its position altered? He slides it back and forth, seeking evidence in dust but without conclusion. Even if it was moved, was it done by the visitor or else last night by Conroy himself, too drunk to notice? Sitting on the edge of the bed that sags wearily beneath him, he puts his head in his hands. There is no truth, no answer. Except that there was no second phone call, and if the bastard said otherwise then that proves him a fake.

He's too disconcerted to continue practising, he feels stifled and needs to go outside. He's in the park later when his mobile rings, it's his agent, Michael. They haven't spoken for a while. Conroy initially keeps walking, almost fooling himself with an air of importance as they discuss business, then feels the need to sit down and finds a vacant bench.

"I'm afraid they've cancelled, David." It was to be a festival appearance in France; Conroy was looking forward to it.

"Then there's nothing in the diary for next season."

"That's how it looks. I'll keep trying. Might need to widen the net a bit."

Conroy knows his agent means: you might need to lower your expectations even further. "I'm working on an interesting new piece," Conroy tells him, wondering how much to say about Klauer, hoping to generate a sense of mystery and anticipation. The gambit fails.

"Let's hope you get a chance to perform it," is all Michael can offer. "Times are hard. There are always new names coming through."

"Like Paul Morrow, for instance."

"I'd hardly call him new."

A boy of three or four has stopped to stare at Conroy, face

of ice-cream-smeared innocence. Poor bastard, Conroy thinks, you don't know what's in store. The mother comes and bundles her child to safety.

"I saw Morrow at Tune Inn," says Conroy.

"I saw him last week. Looking a bit podgy, I thought. Don't reckon he'll be able to do the *enfant terrible* thing much longer."

"How about the recording idea we discussed?"

"Forget it. You know what downloads have done to the market. Look at the pop acts, even they've gone back to touring, only way they can make money. We need to get you on the road again, David. If the South Bank won't have you there's always plan B."

"I thought we were already further down the alphabet than that."

The agent's professional chirpiness suddenly acquires a tone of genuine humanity. "Don't lose hope, David."

In the evening he's got the Klemperer *Missa Solemnis* on the stereo but can't concentrate on the music, he feels uneasy, a stranger in his own home. All the doors and windows are locked, he went round and checked, yet he's still nervous, and every so often pulls at the curtain to see who might be roaming in the darkness outside: the mysterious youths or the confidence trickster who invented them. He's startled by the ringing of his landline, wonders if it's his agent again bringing better news, but it's Claude Verrier who can hear the background music and asks if it's a bad time. Conroy says no and silences Beethoven with a turn of the control.

"I'm just back from Paris," Verrier says brightly, he's been doing business there, makes many such trips. "How's Klauer? Ready for performance?"

"Getting there." Once Conroy has retrieved the slow

movement from his student he'll still need a few more weeks to practise and memorise it all, but he knows he'll get them anyway.

"And what do you think? Have you worked out its secret?"

Conroy perceives a note of irony; Verrier is sufficiently sophisticated to know that music, if it is of any worth at all, is not the bearer of a discoverable message. "The first movement is best," he declares flatly.

"And the finale?" asks Verrier. "Still a *danse macabre*, a black joke?"

"People can interpret it how they like, I don't care for biographical analysis. Too much room for error."

At Verrier's end the sound of a station or air terminal, place of perpetual motion. Then the man's voice. "He really died, though."

"What?"

"I've seen the death certificate. Klauer's buried in Père Lachaise, I went and looked, a very fine headstone though I don't suppose many tourists have noticed it."

A new twist, the latest enharmonic modulation. "What about the newspaper report you showed me, the public meeting in Scotland?"

"What do you think?"

"A coincidence… an impostor."

"The latter more likely. But still not an answer."

Conroy's being teased, manipulated. The possibility occurs to him: all is fake, Verrier is another fraud.

"I've been finding out more about him," says the dealer. "And about the company he kept. Seems Klauer was associated with followers of some obscure philosopher."

"Where have you found this information?"

"They believed in a sort of multiple reality. I don't

understand the details, nonsense anyway I expect, though apparently there are physicists nowadays who reckon there may be something in it."

"What are you saying?"

"He died. And did not die."

"That's ridiculous."

"There's evidence of both."

"The authorities could dig up that grave in Père Lachaise and find an empty box…"

"Or one full of bones," Verrier says calmly, untroubled by the tannoy announcement that almost drowns his voice. "In any case, there's other evidence. I managed to locate a photograph of Klauer, I'll e-mail it to you. Quite a dashing figure, jet-black hair, fine moustache, a studio portrait, background's meant to be trees, I think. He's standing proudly in a white suit with his hat under his arm, could almost be a character out of Proust."

"You said there was other evidence."

"And you didn't let me finish," Verrier says with relaxed firmness. "I also followed up the story of the meeting in Scotland. There was a big political protest at the time about working hours, culminated in a rally in Glasgow that turned into a riot, some historians have called it the closest that Britain came to a communist revolution."

"I've never heard of this."

"Battle of George Square, 1919, look it up for yourself. Klauer was there."

"How can you say that?"

"I found a photo showing a group of protesters, he's in it. I'll send you that, too."

"Then he didn't die."

"The Paris police saw his body, his family identified it. He died."

117

"This is madness."

"Who cares, think of the interest it'll generate. Possibly with a bit more digging we'd find the truth. One truth. But does it matter? Each story works: the tragic composer killing himself and having his identity stolen by a fraudster. Or Klauer the fraudster, discarding his old life to start anew. Let the audience believe both or neither. They want music, not fact."

Conroy should say he will have nothing more to do with this, yet knows it may be the last chance to redeem his career. A choice between two kinds of futility, two forms of weightless oblivion. Klauer dared to have both, to leap and live. "All right," he says. "What happens next?"

1940

Spain

The dignified couple arriving for dinner at the Hotel de Francia are greeted by a low bow from the proprietor and the stern approval of the Generalissimo whose hand-tinted photograph glowers from the wall behind. "Good evening once again," Senor Suner says to his clients with unctuous cordiality, adopting imperfectly but adequately their native French. "Would monsieur and madame care for their usual table?" It has been theirs only twice before but that is enough to establish a tradition; with a snap of his fingers, Senor Suner summons Pablo, the waiter, and tells him in Spanish to prepare for the two guests in the dining room.

"We will be joined by others," the grey-haired Frenchman breaks in, a man imposing in both manner and dress, with the air of a businessman and a wife of comparable age whose mature beauty owes itself not entirely to good connections with the black market in cosmetics.

Suner, pleasantly surprised at the prospect of further distinguished custom, holds Pablo in check. "A second couple?" he inquires.

"We shall see," the Frenchman replies cryptically, then to his wife says, "Yvette, would you mind if I have a word with our host?" She follows Pablo to the dining room, the swinging open of the curtained glass door briefly releasing the impertinent crackle of a gramophone; then when it is closed, Monsieur Carreau says quietly to Suner, "A group of refugees left Banyuls this morning, intending to cross the border."

"Jews?"

"Mostly, yes; also some agitators. The French police know about them. They don't have exit visas."

Suner follows it all perfectly well, given that the scenario is an everyday occurrence, yet rubs his chin at his guest's last remark. "The police let them go up the mountain, though they lack visas?"

Carreau nods. "The civil guard on this side have also been informed. The refugees will be brought to your hotel to stay overnight, then returned."

This is unexpected news. Suner had immediately known, when Monsieur Carreau spoke the other night about "shipping interests", exactly what was meant by the term, the present major item of cross-border trade being people, usually on their way through Spain to Lisbon and then America. The restaurant of his small hotel, in a fishing town notable only for its strategic location, is the regular haunt of under-cover Gestapo men, informers and fugitives, all offered a warm welcome and a hearty meal as long as they can pay for it. But Suner is not used to having his establishment serve as a detention centre. "Who'll pay the bill?" he asks bluntly.

"They are persons of means," Carreau assures him, unable to conceal a note of disgust at such plebeian concerns. "You will not be left out of pocket."

"Then I shall assist the authorities in whatever way I can," Suner avers, touching his moustache where a bead of sweat has lodged, and bowing once again when monsieur moves towards the dining-room door. "Pablo will be pleased to tell you about tonight's dishes, and may I cordially recommend the sea bass."

Such pretensions are typical of Suner and the grimy pension he runs. Monsieur Carreau finds the dining room almost deserted; a young couple huddle in one corner, furtively studying the menu, while in another a gaunt man sits alone with a glass of wine, fingering the stem with a jilted look that could be the poor mask of a spy. Carreau's "usual" table is out of earshot, conveniently close to the gramophone that on his last visit he requested to be turned down. Pablo must have remembered; it might on this occasion be necessary to ask for a raising of volume. Yvette watches her husband's approach impassively. "Have you decided yet?" he asks her, sitting down.

"The waiter said something about fish and I nodded, then he went away. I don't know if that constituted an order."

Carreau laughs and takes her hand which lies on the crumb-specked table. "Darling," he says fondly, but the disdainful lowering of her eyes makes him trail off.

Yvette listens to the music, murmuring half-forgotten lyrics to the dance band's melody, then stops and in a low voice says, "When do you think they'll get here?"

Carreau isn't sure. "I hear that the walk over the mountains can take ten, maybe twelve hours. Depends how fit they are. And how long the police hold them."

The door springs open; it is a new group of diners, all Spanish in appearance: two men in suits, a smartly dressed woman, a boy of nine or ten. The waiter comes and speaks to them rapidly and with familiarity; Yvette is unable to follow but Carreau listens carefully, and seeing his wife's anxiety says softly to her, "It's not them. We'll know when we see them."

Outside, in the lobby, Senor Suner is speaking quietly on the telephone to the local chief of police. "Yes, Juan, I have rooms for them, but I hope this isn't going to be a regular occurrence. I don't want my hotel being turned into a prison."

And at the other end of the line, the police chief momentarily puts his hand over the mouthpiece to tell the deputy waiting at his desk, "Take them now." There they are, sitting on wooden chairs in his office, five women, a teenage boy and an overweight spectacled gentleman with a black leather briefcase at his feet, all exhausted from their walk and dumbfounded by their treatment. It is as if the rules have suddenly been changed, just for them.

Yvette flicks away a crumb from the tablecloth. "You do promise me they'll go free?"

"Of course," Carreau nods. "That's the arrangement." He leans closer to his wife. "We're dealing with small-town minor functionaries; the only thing they understand is the gleam of gold. Everybody'll get what they want."

"But the refugees…"

"They want to leave France illegally and we're helping them do it."

"That's not how it must seem to them right now."

"It's the way it has to be." The music stops, and while Pablo goes to replace the record on the gramophone, Carreau glances cautiously towards the silent man with the wine glass. Only when an operatic aria strikes up does he resume speaking.

"You know I'm doing this for you, Yvette, don't you? All these years, all the searching and gathering, all the running and hiding, it's been for you."

"I know that's what you think, Louis."

"It's what we both know. And now we shall add another piece, we shall draw another step closer. It's the only way. He needs something we can give, he owns something we want."

Yvette looks at him with time-worn sadness. "But a step closer to what, Louis? To happiness? To the grave? You say it's all about protecting me…"

"Yes," he snaps, unable to suppress his impatience. "It's about not letting them do to you what they did to Pierre."

"And I thank you for it," she whispers, "you know I do, I always have. But we're getting old. You seem as determined as ever to go on, you'll never rest until you've put every single piece of the jigsaw together; yet I, Louis, I am tired. If they caught me right now, yes, even if that fellow over there with his empty glass should turn out to be one of them, and if he should come at me with a dagger as soon as we get the documents, you know, Louis, I'm not even sure I'd have the strength to fight. Perhaps I'd really want him to slit my throat, perhaps I'd feel relief at last. I never asked for any of this…"

"I know, darling." Carreau takes her hand again. "But you're the one Pierre chose. No one can alter the path of destiny."

It is a word she has heard too many times. Walking as a young woman in the park nearly thirty years ago, waiting for Pierre to arrive, the word was as thrilling as the big wheel they rode on; destiny meant marriage to a genius, or so she thought. What she got instead were a few relics: a piano score, a lock of hair, the fragile orchid he wore that terrible day – she even thought she could see a spot of blood on it. And the letters, the warnings, the strange and threatening events that Louis, her brave warrior, arrived to rescue her from. He's been rescuing her ever since. Her life has been a long and wearying journey over a mountain, with no indication of who her pursuers really are, or why they want to harm her.

"What's happening to those poor Jews," she murmurs, "is what I've had to endure."

"Then you have to stay quick-witted and alert, like them."

Pablo brings their food; the sea bass is a fish much like any other, made palatable to Louis by the wine that accompanies it, while Yvette finds solace in the succession of records that whirr themselves to completion on the machine beside her.

"*The Magic Flute*," she says at one point. It's the Queen of the Night's aria; tears come to her eyes.

"It's beautiful," Louis says politely, though to his ear it is indistinguishable in quality from whatever he tapped his toe to not long before.

"Pierre always used to say to me…"

"I know, darling, you've told me. He always used to say that in *The Magic Flute* everything's the wrong way round: it's Sarastro who seems evil and the Queen of the Night who's wronged. Yes, that was very wise."

From the lobby beyond the dining-room door, a minor commotion can be heard, of people entering at the command of a raised voice.

"They're here," says Yvette, and Carreau nods.

They are being made to sign the hotel register: Suner, with all the dignity of his station, is pointing an ink-blackened finger-tip at the place where the first of the refugees begins placing her name, then, when she is finished and steps back sorrowfully from the desk, the others follow. Carina Birman, Dele Birman (sister of above), Sophie Lippmann, Greta

Freund, Henny Gurland, Joseph Gurland (son of above), Dr Walter Benjamin. Suner watches the last of them, the only man in the group, dot the letters of his name with a flourish that looks habitual but wearied. "You're a medical man?"

"A doctor of literature."

"What time did you set off from Banyuls this morning?"

"I didn't," Benjamin says wheezily. "I stayed overnight on the mountain and the others caught up with me."

Suner can see that Walter Benjamin is not a well man. The date of birth on the passport he surrenders shows him to be forty-eight but he's more like sixty. "You could have had a heart attack," Suner says to him.

"I thank you for your solicitude."

The policeman accompanying them gives a cough, reminding Suner that pleasantries are not appropriate now, there is business to be done. "Your rooms," says Suner, pulling open the reservation book's biblical mass and finding the evening's arrangements. "You'll all be doubling up, except for the professor." It is a statement of fact, not a proposal, and having needlessly rechecked the allocations he personally made no more than ten minutes ago, a blessing at this low end of the season, he struts out from behind the desk, keys jangling in his fingers, and calls on José, the porter, who leads the prisoners and their guard upstairs. The luggage they carry is whatever they have managed to haul over the mountain, Dr Benjamin has only his briefcase; though had they been more heavily burdened, José still would not have carried anything for them.

All are to be deposited on the second floor, on a corridor otherwise empty of guests. José opens the first door, then nods at the boy and his mother, who follow the wordless prompt and step inside. The indolent porter leaves the door ajar, the key in place, and the policeman says something in Spanish that all the refugees can understand despite their almost total ignorance of the language. They are not to be locked in, but treated as free, since there is nowhere else for them to go.

The next two rooms are given to the four remaining women, then Benjamin is put in the last. He sees José and the policeman slouch complacently back along the corridor, shuts his door on them and goes to lie on the creaking bed, gazing only briefly at the stained striped wallpaper before closing his eyes, too tired even to remove his shoes or jacket. He thought he had bought his freedom with the papers in his briefcase. Yet his life is over.

Yvette watches her husband calmly finish the fish he has found so insufferably bland, a sip of wine easing its passage down his gullet.

"Aren't you going to say something to the manager?"

"I'll ask him to send the gentleman down to join us."

"But is that wise, Louis?"

Pablo comes past; Carreau detains him and asks for Suner, who soon arrives to see what is wanted.

"They're here, aren't they?" says Carreau, and Suner nods, glancing across at the other diners who know nothing of the latest arrivals. "I'd like to see Dr Benjamin."

Surprised, Suner raises an eyebrow. "You know him?" The Frenchman's impassive response precludes further investigation; instead Suner stoops closer to his ear and says, "Under the circumstances, it would not be appropriate for him to be seen by the clientele…"

"Then I shall go to his room – which number?"

Suner straightens. "Twenty-three. On the second floor. I'll get José to show you…"

"I shall find it," Carreau interrupts. "I can count." He

begins to rise from the table, Yvette asks him if she should come too, but Carreau shakes his head. "There's no need," he says. "It's a simple business arrangement, nothing more. Have some dessert, darling, I'm sure our host will be happy to help you choose." Yvette and Suner watch speechlessly as he makes his way out of the dining room, the glass door closing behind him with an indignant bump, then he treads upstairs to find the scholar whose room is easy to locate, though Benjamin himself proves slow to respond to Carreau's rapping. Eventually a muffled groan can be heard.

"It's me, Carreau," he calls impatiently. The door opens. "My God, you look terrible."

Benjamin's face is grey, his eyelids dark and pouchy, his lips strangely puckered, as if he has been kissing a ghost. He seems on the verge of collapse. "I don't feel well," he says. "My pulse…"

Carreau comes straight inside and closes the door. "Do you have it?" he asks in German.

"What? Yes."

"Then let me see – we have very little time."

Benjamin, bewildered by the rush, goes to sit again on the bed that creaks complainingly beneath his excessive weight. He puts a hand to his forehead. "Are you German, then, like me?"

"No."

"You speak the language fluently."

"As well as you speak French." The remainder of their conversation is to be a mixture of the two, a situation Benjamin is used to: a stateless Berliner exiled in France, now seeking further exile in the United States.

There is a wooden chair in the room, but Carreau does not yet take it. He is glancing at the faded decor, assessing its provincial squalor. "Even worse than the restaurant," he mutters, then to Benjamin, "Well?"

"All in good time, monsieur." The briefcase is beside his feet on the floor. "What I want to know is why we were arrested."

"It wasn't part of the plan."

"I know that. When you said on the telephone that you'd meet me in Portbou I didn't think it would be under these circumstances. Many friends of mine have made exactly the same journey in the last few weeks, completely unhindered."

"New regulations," Carreau says, pulling the chair with a scrape and sitting down. "It's not my fault."

"But the item you want from me was supposed to buy my safe passage, that's what you promised."

"And I still give you that promise. All it takes is a bribe to the police chief here. Give me the book and everything will be taken care of."

Benjamin laughs weakly. "Enough of this masquerade, Monsieur Carreau, or whatever your name is. There's no need to try and restore my hope. I know this is the end, and you'll get what you want, some pieces of paper. Only tell me why they matter so much to you."

Carreau smiles without emotion. "I'm a collector."

"Of Jews for the Gestapo?"

"Of first editions and rare manuscripts."

Benjamin nods. "It's a buyer's market: fascism is so good for the economy."

Carreau cares little for gallows humour. "I'm taking risks on your behalf. Whatever you might think, I'm not a Nazi. I really want to help you."

"And my friends?"

"That was never part of the deal – you didn't tell me you'd

show up with a whole tribe."

Benjamin shakes his head. "I only mean Henny and her son – we met the other four on the mountain, taking the same route."

"And they don't matter? They can go to blazes, is that it? Well, that's most heroic."

Benjamin stares at the bedcover he sits on and says nothing.

"So at least we understand each other. A deal is a deal. You, the woman and her son, as we negotiated. I have the train tickets in my pocket, and valid visas for the three of you."

"*Par toi je change l'or en chemin de fer.*"

"Exactly."

"*Et le paradis en enfer.*"

It takes a moment for Carreau to appreciate that Benjamin is parodying poetry, though he can't place the reference. "I don't deal in heaven and hell, Dr Benjamin, only reality. Now show me the book. It's in your briefcase, I assume?"

Benjamin reaches down and pats the black leather bag. "*Mon chat sur le carreau,*" he says gently, then looks up knowingly at the Frenchman. You remember Baudelaire, don't you?"

"Evidently not as well as you."

"But your *nom de guerre* is code, is it not? The suit in a pack of cards?"

"It's my real name," Carreau says blankly.

"Pity," says Benjamin with a sigh. "It suggested to me so many associations: a diamond, a tile, an intersecting network of oblique lines. Do you know, the Englishman Browne wrote an entire essay…"

"Yes," Carreau cuts him off. "I know. I have an early edition. Now open the briefcase."

Benjamin does as he is ordered, and reaching among

spare clothing and essentials crammed inside, retrieves a slim volume bound in pale calfskin which he passes to Carreau, the collector perusing the gilt-tooled cover for some time before even opening it to read the handwritten title page. He nods with satisfaction.

"I paid a lot of money for that," says Benjamin. "Far too much."

"If that's true then it's just as well you did," Carreau replies without looking up from the elegantly bound manuscript whose pages transfix him.

Benjamin can easily understand the fascination they exert. "We both know what it's like to be bewitched by a rare volume, a chance encounter, one that will certainly never happen again."

"Bewitched?" Carreau echoes, half-listening. "An appropriate choice of word." He closes the book and rests it on his lap. "What made you buy it?"

"Its interesting appearance, a persuasive seller. The contents mean nothing to me."

"Of course."

"Though even what is incomprehensible can have a certain poetic quality."

"For all your talk of Baudelaire you don't strike me as a poet."

"When I was younger I thought I might be one. I even tried hashish, under scientifically controlled conditions."

Carreau laughs. "And what did you discover?"

"That it was never my destiny to be an original creative artist, though I might still be a writer. I went to the island of Capri seeking inspiration, fell in love there, and also bought the item you judge to be so precious. To me it is the embodiment of everything that is lost."

"In other words she turned you down."

"But what about you, sir? Why did you go to such lengths, tracking me among the displaced hordes in Marseilles? When I got your telegram I realised this must be no ordinary book, no average collector looking for bargains in troubled times."

Carreau looks witheringly at him. "You know I have no need to explain myself."

Benjamin, humbled, is reminded that their encounter, unlike the object that prompted it, is entirely about material content, not form. "You promised payment."

"I'm a man of my word." Carreau brings the required travel documents from his pocket.

"Did you know our transit visas would be declared invalid at the border?"

"No, and I didn't know you'd be arrested. But with these papers you should be fine." He pauses, the keys to freedom held tantalisingly in his left hand, while his right rests on the book they almost equal. "You realise, of course, that I didn't get these for nothing. And I still need to come to an arrangement with the chief of police."

"You want more?" Benjamin asks, stunned.

"It's only fair."

"But I have nothing else."

Carreau frowns. "Are you trying to tell me your socks aren't stuffed with gold coins? Or is there perhaps another rare item hiding in that briefcase of yours?"

Benjamin lowers his head. "I'm not a rich man. Only an author and book lover."

"Not a successful author, then? Or at least from a family wealthy enough to support a scholarly son?"

"Not even prestigious enough," says Benjamin, "for my books to have suffered the honour of being burned by the fascists. Though I feel the heat."

There is not a trace of sympathy in Carreau's features. "Tell me, in all your hashish dreams, did you ever foresee a future like this?"

"I foresaw it only when sober. Intoxicated, I was in paradise."

"Better to have stayed there. And do you honestly have nothing left to give?"

"It's the truth, sir."

The travel documents are still poised in Carreau's hand. He purses his lips, reaches out his arm. "Take them."

"Thank you…"

"Just take them." Carreau rises to his feet to give the papers to Benjamin, too weak to leave his bed.

"And the chief of police…?"

"I'll see what I can do. Thank you for the book." He looks at it in his hand, tapping it with satisfaction. "Isn't life hellishly ironic? Good luck to you, sir."

The transaction complete, Carreau leaves the room, and in the silence bequeathed to him, Benjamin continues to stare a while longer at the open briefcase, then stuffs the travel papers inside his jacket and lies back with a sigh. He knows the truth: Carreau is a liar and a fraud. There will be no bribe, no negotiation, the parting good-luck wish was an admission that Benjamin is on his own now. Tomorrow they will all be sent back to France and interned there. Carreau is a cheating non-entity while Benjamin, on the contrary, is a genius and an honest man, completely honest, for it is true: he has nothing. His gold coins have been divided between Henny and Joseph, and they will all still have need of them.

Yvette is relieved to see her husband return; being alone in the dining room under the scrutiny of the lone stranger has been unnerving for her. When Carreau sits down again at the table he blocks the suspicious man's unwelcome line of sight. "Did you get it?" Yvette whispers.

He nods.

"Then where is it?"

"I left it at the desk, Suner's there."

"Is that wise?"

"Don't worry, everything's fine."

She glances beyond his shoulder. "That man's been staring at me."

Carreau doesn't need to look round. "You should be flattered – have you really forgotten what it feels like?"

"Don't mock me, Louis. You get what you want and suddenly everything's a joke. That's typical of you."

He turns and waves to Pablo, who gives a harassed acknowledgment from the other end of the room.

"What about the refugees?" Yvette asks him.

"I told you, I'll have a word with the chief of police, it'll all be sorted by morning."

Pablo attends them with a bow; the bill is paltry and Carreau settles it with a few notes, leaving a large tip. "Thank you, senor, thank you!" The waiter insists on shepherding them out of the dining room to the hotel lobby, where Suner is speaking on the telephone.

"That's right, we need a doctor, one of our guests is feeling ill." Suner looks at Carreau and raises a finger of his free hand to show he is in control of everything. "Get Ramon over here to have a look at him. Yes, he can pay, he's a professor, his lady friend came down not long ago to tell me they need help." Suner reaches below the desk and brings out the calfskin book which he slides without comment across the smooth surface into Carreau's grip; the negotiations continue a little longer before Suner hangs up.

"He can pay?" says Carreau.

"I expect he'll have to, one way or another." Suner gives a hoarse chuckle, amused by the plight these foolish French Jews have thrown themselves into.

Carreau reaches into his jacket for something, cocks an eyebrow in apparent surprise, mutters an impatient self-condemnation and then says to both Suner and Yvette, the two of them equal in their ignorance of his intention, "I must go upstairs briefly." He leaves them standing awkwardly alone.

Suner smiles sympathetically at madame who is looking old and tired. "Would you like to sit down?"

She responds with no more than a dignified lifting of her nose. This little hovel is like the whole of Spain, she can't wait to be out of it, just as soon as her husband can complete his work.

"If madame would like a drink…?"

Nothing the manager might possibly say could make her any less eager to escape. She moves away from the desk, Suner becomes occupied with meaningless paperwork, then absents himself to the adjoining office. Not long afterwards, the dining room door opens. It is the lone stranger who comes out, eyeing Yvette significantly in the instant before she glances aside and focuses her attention on a potted plant on the windowsill, potent object of simulated interest.

"Good evening, madame."

She thinks she hears a German accent embedded in his good French, and cannot avoid his greeting, nor conceal her unease. "Good evening, monsieur."

"How many goodly creatures are there here."

It sounds like some form of code; a relief, because it means he must be looking for someone else. "Monsieur," she says with a polite and final nod as she turns away to examine once more the trailing leaves of the plant.

But he is not to be so easily dismissed. In a whisper close beside her ear he suddenly says, "Take my advice, get out of town, you and your husband. Do it tonight." Startled, she sees the curt bow with which he takes his leave of her.

She is still trying to make sense of it when Louis returns, looking cross. "Come on," he says gruffly.

Suner, alerted by his guest's descent, comes back out of the office and goes to hold open the door for them, attending their every movement like a panting dog, exhorting them to return tomorrow for an even more delicious meal. Once outside in the street, Yvette asks her husband what happened with the professor.

"I offered him some medicine," he says. Then drawing his wife close to his side, he escorts her safely away.

Chapter Five

Paige is in Starbucks with Ella when she gets the call.

"It's David Conroy. There's something we need to discuss. Could we meet?"

She's seen him only once, when she had her first lesson a few days ago, and already he's phoning her. Paige's confusion is obvious to Ella who watches with a mixture of fascination and concern, able to hear the male crackle at her friend's ear. Ella mouths *Who?* and Paige mimes helplessness. The meeting is fixed for later that week, the tutor hangs up and Paige explains.

"But you surely aren't going to…"

"I'm seeing him at the college," Paige says reassuringly.

"He fancies you."

"It's about the piece I'm meant to be learning, that's all. He wants me to give him back the score."

"Hasn't he got one of his own? Can't you drop it off?" Suspicion comes easily to Ella's mind. "How old is he?"

"I don't know, pretty old, in his forties."

"This isn't about music. He arranges extra lessons in college, next thing he's asking you back to his place for some

136

advanced tuition."

Paige won't be treated like a child. "Nothing's going to happen unless I want it to."

"When did you ever know what you want?" Ella says lightly, and Paige's silence chills the atmosphere. "I didn't mean…"

"Forget it."

But the subject has been raised and Ella won't let it go. "Sean got a new job."

"I don't care what he does." Sean was a mistake, like the foetus he made. They'd pretty much split already when she found out. Her body told her what her mind must do: reject everything of him.

"You've got the right attitude, Paige. Ignore them completely, best way to make them feel bad. Cut loose and never go back."

"I'm not playing games."

"But surely you miss him sometimes? Bound to, until you find someone else. Then you make certain he knows."

Paige doesn't want to talk about it, she gazes towards the door of the café and sees two boys entering that she knows from college. Ella registers the distraction and turns to look. One of the boys waves.

"Who are they?" Ella asks.

"I think the tall one's called Rob."

The boys get their order then come to say hello. Introductions are made, the tall one isn't called Rob after all, his friend hides shyly behind a long fringe. Ella invites them to sit.

"Hear about the bust?" says not-Rob to Paige. Police came to the college and arrested an Egyptian violinist who'd been posting offensive remarks online. "He said the British troops deserved to die."

"Then what did he expect?" says Ella.

"Got to have free speech," the shy one offers, possibly wanting some kind of debate about it, but the conversation lapses. Ella restarts it. "Do you know a teacher at college called Conroy?"

"I had him once as accompanist," says the tall one.

"Does he have a reputation?" Ella asks him. "You know, with girl students?" Seeing Paige's reaction she adds, "Just asking."

"I couldn't say," he responds. "Only thing I heard is he had a breakdown in the past, gets moody. One time he got really angry with my mate Harry, swore at him."

Ella folds her arms in vindication.

"What did your mate do to upset him?" Paige asks.

He shrugs. "Nothing."

Paige has to go, she's booked a practice room. Her plan was to work on the Klauer slow movement, there's no need if Conroy wants her to return the score, but she's glad of an excuse to leave Ella with the other two who look to Paige as though they should still be at school. She feels so much older than them all, after what she's been through.

Walking to the college she wonders how it would have turned out if she hadn't miscarried. She's sure she would have aborted it, but can't help imagining the parallel world with an extra life in it. Adoption, perhaps, then years later her daughter finds her, demands to know everything. You work so hard to eliminate mistakes but they always happen.

The practice room is still occupied: peering through the small window in the thick door Paige sees a Chinese girl playing what she guesses to be Rachmaninov, head bent in concentration, right hand leaping gymnastically across the keyboard. It looks dispiritingly perfect. Paige checks her watch then abruptly opens the door on the girl who stops, startled, and immediately apologises for having overrun. Paige tells her it's no problem, drops her bag to the floor and feels the energy being pulled out of her by this clockwork virtuoso who will always be so much better and brought nothing but her talent. She bows and scuttles out.

Klauer is irrelevant but it's the only score Paige has, and rather than perform mechanical exercises or play from memory she prefers the distraction of reading, so she sits and begins. The dark and complex music is appropriate to her mood; the doomed composer's handwriting makes Paige feel as if her fingers are able to touch his across a distance of a hundred years, a span that means nothing. When she played for Mr Conroy he asked what the music made her see, but the images keep changing, she's distracted by thoughts of that idiot Sean, why did Ella have to mention him? She thinks of Mr Conroy's sudden change of mind about the score, wonders what prompted his breakdown, knows there doesn't need to be a reason though people always want a neat answer. Like Klauer, probably he got a bad review from a critic or fell out with his lover so he killed himself, that's how it's meant to work, one thing logically following another, except that his music isn't like that, there seems no connection between the parts, no necessity, only chance.

Why not memorise it anyway? A small, tactical gesture of defiance, her right to play what she likes. She'll never be perfect like the one who was here before but she can still be an artist. She spends her hour working through the movement, repeating each section and imprinting it on her mind and fingers, this song of sadness or joy, pain or triumph, she'll remember it even though she doesn't know what any of it means. At home she continues so that when the time comes for her to see Mr Conroy again a few days later she knows it by heart, though he'll never hear her play.

She arrives for the appointment and knocks the door, he calls for her to enter and she finds him sitting reading. His office looks bare, without a single picture or ornament, the shelves largely empty, giving an impression of transit, or someone living almost entirely inside his own head, with little need for physical comfort or external distraction. He looks up, his glasses catch the light. "Do you have it?" he asks at once.

"The score? Sure."

"Leave it there," he instructs, nodding towards the desk. She deposits it on an empty corner and stands waiting for him to say something else, but he's turning the pages of his book as though having already forgotten she's there. Eventually he looks again and says, "Thanks."

"You said we needed to have a meeting."

"Not really."

She's taken aback. "You made it sound so important."

"An over-reaction."

Whose does he mean, she wonders, feeling increasingly exasperated. "I came here specially for this."

Conroy appears to have some emerging recognition of his own rudeness. "Take a seat," he offers, waving towards a chair and laying aside the open book. "Tell me what you make of the piece."

By now it has suggested so many contradictory pictures: a lullaby sung by a skeleton, an anthem for the broken-hearted, a text message saying "it's over", a stump of flesh expelled in the toilet. "I wonder what he'd have done if he'd lived."

"Klauer? Been a different person. Not the one destined to shoot himself but someone else instead. I think it was going to be a symphony but he didn't get as far as orchestrating it. All we've got is an outline."

A sketch of a life the composer was condemned never to lead. That would be one way of making sense of it: the jumbled image of so many unrealised possibilities.

Conroy says, "The owner of the original manuscript gave me the photocopy on the understanding that I wouldn't share it with anyone. He wants to protect his investment."

The explanation is prosaic; Conroy's face implies something more he wants to say, yet doesn't.

"What should I be practising instead?"

He's not listening, he thinks for a moment then suddenly asks, "What would you consider the most important thing in your life?"

She guesses he wants her to say music. "Family and friends. Being healthy."

"You lose those things."

"Sometimes. That's why they're important."

"Training to be a performer isn't like studying to be an engineer or a geographer. It's about your whole life, what you are as a person. There mustn't be distractions. Do you have a boyfriend?"

Paige feels her face redden. "Yes," she lies.

"Is he a musician?"

"No. What about your partner?"

He looks surprised. "Who?"

"You said your partner left you. When I had my lesson."

"I did? It was inappropriate of me. Did you find it inappropriate?"

"I thought it was a strange thing to say at a first lesson."

"I only remember telling you to read Adorno. He's important, you know." Conroy ruminates. "How about *Humoreske*?"

"What?"

"Schumann. As a study work."

"Instead of Klauer? But I'll need another twentieth-century piece won't I?"

"Forget the syllabus, you came here to study because you love playing."

"I want a degree though."

"I'll take care of it. You've got talent, that's what matters. We need to be flexible. Do you know *Humoreske*? No? One of the movements has a third stave with a theme you're meant to hear inside your head, but not play. What do you make of that? When I recorded it some years ago, I thought of the hidden melody, exactly as Schumann instructs. I wonder how many people could hear it when they listened to the CD. I wonder if anyone even listened."

Perhaps it's only because the boy in the café mentioned a breakdown, but a suspicion is growing in Paige's mind that Mr Conroy is slightly unhinged. Not simply artistic or eccentric, but a bit mad. "Would I need to think of the hidden tune too?"

Conroy shrugs. "If it's written then you've got to obey the instruction. Did I tell you why she left me?"

"You said you got back from a concert tour and she'd walked out, taken all her belongings."

"Yes," Conroy reminds himself, "like she was never there. Has it ever occurred to you how easily a person can disappear from the world?"

She's only been struck by how easy it is for new ones to appear.

"You're still too young to think about these things. Life for you is the future, it's something that's going to happen. Eventually you realise it's already over, though you didn't notice at the time. I died, you know."

This really is mad. "What do you mean, died?"

"On stage. It wasn't a bad performance, in some ways it was one of my best. But it was when my life stopped being in the future and started being in the past. Did you know I recorded several CDs? Great reviews, then the label dropped me. That's what Klauer could have looked forward to, having his moment of success then going out of fashion."

"At least he'd have had his moment."

"Did the police interview you?"

Paige guesses he's talking about the Egyptian violinist. "I never knew anything about it."

"An officer came to my house and searched it, I didn't realise what was going on, I left him upstairs undisturbed. Look what I found afterwards." From his pocket he extracts something small and round, a shiny object that he shows to Paige, expecting her to take it from his outstretched fingers. "I don't care if they spy on me, I've got nothing to hide."

She looks at it, wondering if this is a joke, a provocation, or just the way that some people react when a relationship fails and for a little while they break adrift from reality. "It's only a button battery," she says.

1941

New York

The story is told of a marvellous automaton with the appearance of a Turk seated at a chessboard, a hidden mechanism enabling it to move and play. In fact it was operated by a concealed hunchback pulling strings. Hannah Arendt thinks of it as she sits in the respectably shabby reception area of the Institute for Social Research. She arrived here in New York with her husband only a few days ago; before that they were in Lisbon for three months trying to arrange the crossing. Plenty of time to ponder the costumed robot that wins every game through trickery.

It's a sunny June morning and she can hear the rumble of traffic outside. The secretary offers her coffee, says cheerfully that Dr Adorno will be with her soon, but Hannah declines the drink, she can taste bitterness already. Her visit is not for Adorno's sake, she despises the man. She is here because of

Walter Benjamin.

Friendship is considered an abbreviation of the customary distance between people; yet it need do nothing to alter the quantity of separation, only its quality. Hence the paradox that the greatest mark of friendship, as of enmity, is silence. When Hannah saw Walter in Marseilles, the two of them having been brought together again through the frantic scramble for visas, she was shocked at how haggard and distressed he was. In an atmosphere of urgency and desperation he entrusted to her a collection of his own papers, instructing that if she reached America first then she must take them to Adorno. Nothing else was said. The Institute for Social Research, originally based in Frankfurt, had supported Benjamin's work; these same Marxist scholars tried to bring him to New York to join them in exile. Hannah appreciates their exertion; but unlike hers it was a collective effort, and the room where she waits is pervaded by the same oppressive aura of bureaucratic uniformity. The coffee table has the Institute's publications available for perusal; the chair she sits on is made neither for work nor comfort, only for a condition of delay that everyone hopes will not be too protracted. What exactly do they do here? Much of their labour, she has heard, is invested in making applications to charitable funding bodies.

In Lisbon she read Walter's writings, copied and discussed them, above all his essay 'On The Concept Of History', a work he must have considered a kind of testament. There the mechanical Turk serves as metaphor for historical materialism, a theory supposedly able to demonstrate, despite all contrary evidence, that humanity is progressing towards a better state. Free the captive hunchback, Walter seemed to be saying, discard the ridiculous machine; yet nine months ago he was beaten by it. He thought he could enter Spain without a French exit visa; other refugees had done it before, unmolested. But on just that day, the one he chose for his escape, the rules were different. On the chessboard the king lies toppled while the automaton withdraws its triumphant arm, the expression on its face unaltered.

Theodor Adorno comes in, short and bald, even uglier than she remembers, with his big dark eyes and upper-bourgeois air of entitlement some women supposedly find attractive. He looks surprised. "You?"

"Didn't the secretary tell you I was here?"

"She said there was a Frau Blücher to see me, I didn't realise it was you."

Names these days have become as fluid as nationalities; the dark-suited scholar who scrutinises her so circumspectly used to be called Wiesengrund until he dropped his father's surname, blatant as a yellow star, replacing it with the more attractive Italian one that had been his mother's. Hannah will never forgive him for that; her excuse is the more conventional one of recent remarriage, previously she was Frau Stern. They are both in their mid-thirties yet Wiesengrund-Adorno has the manner of an elder statesman puffed up by surroundings he considers prestigious: surplus floor-space on the campus of Columbia University. He looks at her with eyes devoid of desire; Hannah knows how philosophers make love and how they express contempt, explaining either as the fruit of reason. She sees his curiosity drawn exclusively towards the folder of documents on her lap. She explains their origin.

"We should go to my office."

The state of emergency that grips the world is not the exception but the rule: following Adorno along the corridor is little different from appearing at the consulate in order to be assessed for survival by a bland functionary who tells everyone not to take it personally. Humanity is superseded by the reconfiguration of paperwork meant to replicate it, by rules that must be followed, the rules of an artificial second nature. Walter Benjamin was to have been saved by some headed notepaper the Institute sent him, showing his own name among the listed members. Hannah Arendt's passport has been her political activism; a stipend from the Zionist Organization of America pays for the room she and her husband have rented on West 95th Street, where the landlady is a vegetarian bird-watching hiker who forbids smoking. In Europe that would make her a fascist; in America things are different, apparently.

Teddie Adorno goes to sit behind his desk while Hannah Arendt perches on the chair facing him, crossing her legs beneath the precious folder. Is this how she seduced Heidegger, he wonders, while for Hannah it is another round in the chess match. Walter told her to bring the papers to Adorno because he was the one man likely to publish them. It was Hannah whom Walter trusted as a genuine friend; she is witness and bearer of the legacy.

"I have something you should see," Adorno tells her. From the drawer of his desk he brings out a battered correspondence box stuffed with letters and retrieves a creased postcard, sliding it across the table into Hannah's view. She stares at the neat French script.

In a situation without escape, I have no other choice but to finish it all. It is in a little village in the Pyrenees where no one knows me that my life must end.

She's heard already, of course, how Walter and his companions were detained in a hotel where Walter apparently took an overdose of his own heart medicine. But not this final message.

I ask you to pass on my thoughts to my friend Adorno and

to explain to him the situation in which I have found myself.
There is no more time for me to write all the letters I would
have wished to write.

She is astonished, also instinctively doubtful. "This is not
Walter's hand."

"He wrote the message for Henny Gurland who was with
him in Portbou. She thought it best to memorise and destroy it,
then wrote this copy once she was safe."

Terror heightens and perfects the faculty of memory; the
most exact antithesis to thought is unlimited freedom of writing,
eliminating its value in the same way alchemists feared the
easy manufacture of gold would render their discovery futile.
Teddie watches her re-read the postcard and can imagine it
the centrepiece of a Hollywood dramatisation, sentimental
history vignetted to the accompaniment of violins. She's never
liked him, not since his criticism of her first husband's work
on the philosophy of music. She's no longer even married to
the man but still bears the grudge. Somehow, Adorno thinks,
Frau Blücher cannot appreciate the dialectic of memoration
and forgetfulness.

"Now you should read this," she says, leaning forward to
place the folder on his desk.

"Later, of course."

"The first piece is rather short, I should like to hear your
thoughts."

She watches as he opens the folder and lifts the uppermost
item, 'On The Concept of History'. The story of an automaton
rigged to win every game: the theory of progress. Walter had
been trying to write a book about nineteenth-century Paris
but there were only voluminous notes, disconnected sketches;
material the self-styled Institute for Social Research could
never use since it failed to conform to their or anyone else's

prefabricated system. Walter's was the sort of mind the Nazis would have delighted in liquidating.

Adorno's initial perusal is a swift assessment of names and references; to Hannah he looks, with his glasses perched on his broad bald forehead, like someone marking an end-of-term paper. Lines from Brecht bear testimony to the unfortunate delinquency of Benjamin's thought, his willingness to embrace shock, populism, mysticism. Each numbered section a mere paragraph or two, a general deficiency of analysis and rigour, one describes a painting Adorno knows, Klee's *Angelus Novus*. Walter owned it, paid a thousand marks for it. The angel is the figure of history, looking retrospectively at chaos and disaster: we are blown backwards into the future by a tempest. This is the painting that will later come to Adorno, rolled in a cardboard tube, just like the postcard and the essay he will not publish, an act that Arendt will publicly condemn. Already the years are filled with nowness from the end of time.

"This is remarkable," Adorno murmurs after a while. "He has clarified so much of what we discussed."

Envy, Benjamin writes, is something we feel most strongly, not towards what was or will be, but with regard to what might have been. "People we could have talked to, women who could have given themselves to us." His suicide note, if genuine, appears to express this envy most starkly: "all the letters I would have wished to write." In an introduction that Arendt will provide for a collection of his essays published in 1968, she will liken Benjamin to his own description of Kafka: "once he was certain of eventual failure, everything worked out for him." Alike too, though, in their apparent unenviousness, a purity of vision evoking the austere generosity of universal friendship without specific object, a quality sometimes termed saintliness. Benjamin's final sentence would then express unregretful humility: words that need never be said. History is ultimately redemptive.

But what of the world the rest of us inhabit: the world of envy? Then it no longer matters what was, is, or will be, but rather what could have been, what might be. In a world driven by envy, history becomes the multiple image of its alternatives, a condition inextricably linked with pastiche. To escape is impossible, to ignore is to surrender; Adorno is sufficiently unfree of envy to appreciate his deceased colleague's insight.

"I know you can't possibly agree with any of it," Hannah says.

Adorno looks up, as mystified by her latest comment as by her first appearance. "Why do you say that?"

"Because he is arguing against everything that you and this so-called Institute claim to stand for."

It is the kind of crude rhetoric he has come to expect from a woman whose philosophical career has advanced itself in men's beds as much as in seminar rooms. She has given him five minutes to glance at the essay then insists he should feel defeated by it. In those five minutes he has probably understood more than she managed in the whole of her ferry crossing. He has seen numerous drafts and fragments of Walter's Paris project; it appeared at one stage as though the proposed work would consist almost entirely of quotations, with hardly any theoretical explanation at all. At least this final essay shows where he was heading.

Since arriving in America, Adorno has divided his time between the Institute and a publicly funded investigation into the state of radio broadcasting. He is planning to write a book with Max Horkheimer explaining how the Enlightenment gave rise to its opposite, a form of mass deception nowadays propagated by a thriving culture industry. It will be published in 1947 and read by hardly anyone. Arendt will publish *The Origins Of Totalitarianism* four years later and it will make her internationally famous. He reads aloud another part of the essay. "Within three decades they managed virtually to erase the name of Blanqui." Arendt stares blankly at him. "You know how strangely fascinated he was by Blanqui?"

This is a move on the board that Hannah has not been anticipating.

Adorno explains, "He wrote very excitedly to me about a forgotten book he'd found, *L'Éternité par les astres*. He saw it as profoundly important to his project."

Planets where history goes differently, worlds created out of sheer envy and boredom, a universe where an alternative 1941 is happening right now to participants unaware of their genericity. Destiny, chance, fate: all are illusory in the magic-lantern show of history, the eternal now that makes everything feel new when really it is unconscious repetition. Adorno hears this universe every time he turns on the radio and is subjected to the latest dance tune, no different from the last. Modern existence is combinatorial, a rearrangement of terms robbed of meaning, and Walter was trying to reinvigorate meaning through intellectual montage; all he lacked was a coherent theory. The essay shows that had he been able to come to America, then together they would have elucidated that theory. Contingencies preclude that happy outcome, and this is why Adorno will not publish. It has nothing to do with personalities or the distasteful mess of life.

Arendt rises. "I have fulfilled my duty to my friend. Now you must respect your own obligation."

"He didn't give these papers in order that they would be made public in a wholly uncritical way. We shall have to look closely at all of this. Perhaps there is something that can be saved from the disaster."

"It's saved already."

"Salvation is an immanent concept."

"Like damnation?"

The cruellest twist is what both already know: that immediately after Walter killed himself, the Spanish authorities had a change of heart and decided the Jews need not have been detained after all, they would not be deported back to France, but were instead free to travel onwards as they had intended. Had he not given in to despair, Walter would have reached America with the others.

Adorno says, "He sent me a draft introduction for his Paris book, where he talked about Blanqui's absurd cosmology. False histories offering infinite variety at the expense of value, multiplied lives worthless as dust. A desire for everything that instead yields nothing; the essence of modernity."

"You could have done more to save him. We must at least make sure he did not die in vain."

Adorno shakes his head. "He has already done that for us. In death he asserted the uniqueness of existence. There is only one world, and it is the world where our friend took his life. That he took it for no reason, that he need not have left his great work unfinished and in ruins, serves only to heighten the preciousness of what we are denied."

Chapter Six

Paige is getting ready to go to college, standing in the living room of her flat hurriedly finishing a cup of coffee when her phone rings.

"Hello, Paige?"

His tone's friendly but she doesn't recognise the voice. "Who is this?"

"My name's Julian Verrine. I'm trying to get in touch with David Conroy. Do you know where I could find him?"

"Why should I?"

"You're his student, aren't you?"

"Not any more. They told me he's on sick leave."

He chuckles. "Is that what they're calling it? No, David's on another of his walkabouts, he does it now and again, goes AWOL and leaves everyone else to pick up the pieces."

"You're from the college?"

"I was meant to be arranging some performances, can't get hold of him. Has he contacted you?"

"I heard he'd had a breakdown."

"He'll come up for air soon enough, always does."

"How did you get my number?"

"David thinks very highly of you, says you're the best he's seen in years. A bit rough round the edges but definite star quality: his exact words."

"Really? I'm amazed."

"That's why he gave you that piece to learn."

"The Klauer?"

"You still have it?"

"No."

He pauses. "We should talk. You're obviously quite a talent."

"Not exactly ready for the big time yet," she laughs, warmed by flattery.

"There are opportunities even for someone at your stage. Let's say we meet and throw a few ideas around."

"But…"

"How do you feel about crossover?"

Does he think he can make her a pop star? "I don't know."

"I'm looking to showcase some new talent, young hopefuls, you appreciate I'm thinking aloud here, really we should talk. Lunch tomorrow? Even if it goes nowhere you'll at least get a decent meal out of me."

And in a moment it's all arranged, she hangs up thinking this could be a psycho stalker or the biggest break of her life.

It's three weeks since she showed up for a lesson with Mr Conroy only to be told he was unwell. Her tutor since then has been Mrs White, and when Paige arrives to see her she's still thinking about Verrine's call, wondering whether to mention it. They're working on Chopin's Scherzo in C sharp minor, Mrs White wants Paige to play it at a student recital later in the term. Mrs White is nearly at retirement age, has a grown-up daughter in Australia and a son who's an anaesthetist; she's fat and motherly, in a purple angora sweater with her spectacles hanging from a chord on her ample bosom. Paige can't imagine ever being like her.

"You're still using your old fingering," Mrs White points out, interrupting Paige's performance, saying it as if she were disapproving of the amount of salt being added to a pot of soup.

"Sorry," says Paige. She's been practising it exactly the way Mrs White wants, different from the fingering in the score and anything that would have occurred to Paige naturally, but supposedly better. Mrs White can do her own fingering perfectly and expects every one of her students to do the same. Paige tries again, they get along for a page or two.

"No ritardando there," Mrs White reminds her. She chose the Chopin Scherzo for Paige to learn because, she said, it shouldn't only be for those "big muscly boys", and the unwanted image that came to Paige's mind was of Sean, now going out with someone else according to social media and more particularly Ella. The Scherzo alternates between the muscly stuff and what Mrs White calls the "feminine" passages: Chopin, she maintains, was deeply in touch with his feminine side. These episodes are like flowing water, ripples on a lake; the other parts are solid rock. But whenever Paige tries to pursue this imagery she only ends up with Sean, herself, and the foetus.

The family photographs in Mrs White's comfortably furnished room are more prominent than the piano that serves as support for several of them. The anaesthetist is seen in various stages: nappies, school uniform, geeky graduate, nervous bridegroom. The daughter looks like a younger Mrs White, embracing her own children in sharp antipodean sunlight, declaring success to the world, though Mrs White herself has an old-fashioned modesty that is immediately comforting. Her lessons typically begin with tea and end with biscuits ("I mustn't," she always insists, taking a Hobnob from the china plate). Mrs White says she never had any ambitions to be a soloist, would have liked to have done more touring as a chamber musician but had two children to bring up and, well, had to make choices.

Paige has been asked to do one of the watery bits again, she's got to get the fingering right otherwise that water's going to pour out of her hands and make a puddle on the floor. All very well hacking away at the rocks but they're mountains in the background, need to look at what's in front. And Paige thinks of Julian Verrine, his invitation to what she supposes should be called a business lunch. Can't help imagining herself on Classic FM bashing through crowd-pleasing double octaves and to hell with getting the trickles right. Definite star quality. Sean opens the newspaper and sees her looking glamorous in a full-page interview. Wishes he'd never hurt her.

Mrs White says they should take a short break because she can see that Paige is getting tired. Very important not to overstretch the tendons. She refills Paige's teacup and says she's had a letter from Sarah about the mission, Paige is never good at keeping up with soap-opera but knows from previous lessons that the daughter does some kind of religious work, Mrs White is a loyal church-goer and exudes a serenity that Paige envies though also doubts. All very well to have faith yet what if it's false? Paige would never discuss it with her, but if the miscarriage came up she knows Mrs White would say it's in heaven, the little cabbage stalk grew wings and became an angel, when really it never had any life except a potential one that got burned like old paper.

Paige declines a Jaffa Cake and asks, "Have you heard anything about Mr Conroy?"

Mrs White shakes her head earnestly.

"Is it true he's gone missing?"

"So it would appear. Some fear the worst."

"You mean harming himself?"

"He tried it before, you know, when he had a breakdown a few years ago. Such a common story, artists cracking under the strain. So easy to become isolated and obsessive. And it all started so well for him, I remember when people were seriously calling him a new Pollini. But that was a long time ago."

"Beaten by his own demons."

"He certainly made a fine job of sabotaging his career though who can say how things would have turned out otherwise? You know how heavily the odds are stacked against any kind of success, Paige. First there has to be complete mastery of technique, no one would question David's, in his day he was astonishing. And sensitive interpretation, again he had it, even if his readings were a little clinical. Then luck, David got his break when John Ogden had to cancel a performance and they wanted a last-minute replacement. But once you've got an audience you have to hold on to it, and that means connecting. I don't think David ever truly connected with the public. I think he despised them, because really he despised himself."

Paige wants to know more but it's time to resume work. Her mind keeps wandering and her playing is sub-standard, Mrs White can sense it and soon calls a halt.

"Perhaps you didn't get enough sleep," she says kindly.

Paige is thinking about the meeting with Julian Verrine, wondering what to wear. "Can I ask you a question?"

"Of course, dear."

"How good do you really think I am?"

Mrs White answers without hesitation. "You've got huge

potential."

"I'm not talking about that." Potential, Paige knows, is something that gets incinerated. "I mean now."

The teacher's beneficence remains undimmed though her response is evasive. "There's a difference between performing for one person in a room and a thousand in a concert hall."

"I want to know if I can connect."

"You need to do the other things first: technique, interpretation, projection."

"I'm twenty years old, there are pianists younger than me giving Prom concerts."

"Yes, and Liszt was touring when he was twelve, you missed your chance at being a child prodigy. But as a mature artist you're not yet fully formed. A child could learn the part of King Lear, but would he understand it?"

"You're saying I don't have enough life experience?" Paige is thinking: if only you knew.

"Yes, I suppose that's what I'm saying. If you're asking me about show business then it doesn't matter, the younger the better, as long as there are no wrong notes. A lot of concert-goers hear Beethoven no differently at fifty than they did when they were twenty so that's all the more reason for it not to matter, they like to see someone young and pretty on stage doing something they can't do but wish they could. Given the right PR you could probably have a career like that tomorrow, though it wouldn't last long."

Paige wants to ask Mrs White about Verrine, has she heard of him? She says nothing.

"We're not going down that road," Mrs White says with maternal firmness. "We do things the right way, college concerts and competitions, no jumping the queue."

The teacher offers more tea and biscuits for consolation but what Paige reads in Mrs White's words is a simple message: you're not good enough. She asks, "Did Mr Conroy say anything about me?"

"David and I have never had much to say to each other about anything."

"You don't get on?"

"We all have our own kinds of artistic temperament. Put it this way, the reason why David never did chamber performances was that he couldn't find players who'd put up with him. A soloist in everything."

"I heard that his wife left him."

Mrs White looks surprised. "Wife? He's never been married."

"Or his partner. He said she walked out on him. Not long before I started."

"He's always lived alone."

"But he said it."

"It simply isn't true."

"Then he lied to me?"

Mrs White sighs. "He has quite serious mental issues, you realise."

"Delusions?"

"That's what it sounds like. He's always been very private but one thing I can say for certain is that no woman would ever have been able to live with David Conroy."

Paige is stunned. She mentally replays her encounters with Conroy, instantly reinterprets them, knowing that nothing he said can be trusted. Her star quality is no longer definite, there is only roughness around the edges. She's gripped by a sickening dizziness. What about Julian Verrine, has he also been deceived by Conroy's fantasies? Paige wants to tell Mrs White but it's too late, the teacher is looking at the clock, lifting the biscuit plate, smiling to indicate that time's up and she has another appointment. With rising nausea Paige goes out and along the corridor, pushing between other students to reach the staircase, hurrying as she goes down to the entrance hall, her throat dry as stone, tears gathering. She's beside the glass case with its celebration of the famous and the dead, the remembered few, the ones of whom it's been decided that they mattered after all. She wants to smash the bloody thing.

She tries calling Ella but it goes onto voicemail and Paige hangs up, she starts texting then quickly deletes it. Who gives a shit what Conroy did or didn't say, or what Mrs White thinks? You've got to believe in yourself as an artist, this is what Paige tells herself, though the voice she hears isn't really hers, it's the voice of someone she'd rather be, someone who could genuinely believe. The louder voice, her own, is saying: you've fucked it up, you should have listened to your parents. You're good but not great. Do you really want to earn a living playing cocktail bars and wedding receptions?

She needs air and daylight, goes through the revolving door onto the steps and stands feeling the breeze, breathing deeply until the sickness leaves her. The sound of traffic calms her, movement of distant pedestrians, spectacle of life's insignificance.

"Hey, Paige."

She turns and sees in his regular spot the skinny protester with his placard on a pole. Only him today. No hat this time, his brown hair is untidy and he needs a shave but the look suits him. Still can't remember his name.

"You OK?" he asks.

"Where are the others?"

"Didn't show."

She goes over to him, looks at the placard with its painted

slogan. "Why do you do this?"

"Because I want change."

"And you think this can make a difference? Doesn't change happen anyway?"

He starts telling her the kind of idealistic stuff he must say to everyone, she zones out and watches his teeth, sees a tiny white spot of saliva find its way onto his lip and stay there like a pearl, wonders what it would be like to be kissed by him. Eventually she interrupts. "Aren't there better places to make a protest than outside a music college?"

"Sure, but I don't want to miss lectures."

"Revolution has its limits, right?"

He laughs, she joins in.

"Better go."

"Bye, Paige."

The conversation has lifted her mood, she walks home thinking about her meeting, it'll probably go nowhere but you never know. It isn't down to Conroy or Mrs White or her mum and dad: it's about people like Julian Verrine. Again she plays the fantasy of Sean opening the newspaper, a photograph of her at the keyboard.

Next day she arrives promptly at the restaurant, a place she's never been in, popular with media types by the look of it, stylishly minimalist like a picture in a magazine. The waiter sees her lingering at the entrance and comes to attend; she gives Verrine's name and is taken to a table already occupied by a slim man in his thirties wearing a light grey suit. He stands and greets her warmly.

"Paige, great to meet you, so glad you could come."

He has a firm handshake, deep suntan, finely trimmed beard and an expensive looking watch. Later, when Paige tries to describe him, she'll find that this is all she can say about

Julian Verrine.

"How's the piano playing?" he asks brashly, she tells him she's studying Chopin and he nods approvingly. "Can't do better than that. David's never been too much of a fan, though." Immediately they have alighted on the subject of their common acquaintance. "Heard anything?"

"My new teacher worries he might have harmed himself."

"Let's hope not," Verrine says earnestly. "It would be so out of character."

The waiter brings water and offers them a selection of bread rolls, a piece of theatre that puts her in mind of Mrs White's comments about show business. It occurs to Paige that as a pianist she's training to be a kind of retail assistant, serving up musical morsels with a flourish. Verrine orders a glass of red wine, Paige sticks to water. She asks him how exactly he knows Conroy.

"We go back a long way."

"You're his agent?"

"I've helped set up quite a few of his performances. Not an impresario as such, but I have contacts. That's what it's all about, you know. Contacts." His moisturised skin creases easily into a smile as he raises his glass to toast their new partnership. "Now, tell me about Klauer."

The sudden change of topic takes her aback. "What about him?"

"You still have the piece?"

"I gave my copy back to Mr Conroy. He told you about it?"

Verrine cuts into his roll, disembowels it and pushes some of the white fluff into his mouth, scrutinising Paige who for a moment sees his eyes flick to her breasts before he takes a sip from his glass to wash down the bread. "Did you play all of it?"

"Only the slow movement."

"Odd case from what I hear. Shot himself and survived, something like that."

"I wouldn't know."

The waiter comes again, the next stage of the performance, inviting them to order. They haven't looked at their menus; Verrine glances at his and opts for steak, Paige finds her attention falling more on the prices than the elaborate descriptions, hopes she hasn't misinterpreted the arrangement, and orders a risotto involving morel mushrooms and pine kernels. She has no idea where such things come from or how they're harvested, they seem to exist only for places like this.

"Chopin, eh?" Verrine resumes. "Poor fellow's buried all over the place, heart's in Warsaw and the rest of him's in Paris, though it's what he wanted, apparently. Know about his eyes?"

"Where are they buried?"

"Paris, I presume. But no one knows what colour they were. Liszt wrote that they were blue, others swore they were brown, some say hazel. Rotted away to dust now, so we'll never find out." It's a sad and distasteful image but Verrine doesn't notice Paige's reaction or else doesn't care, instead he pursues the thought. "So many things we can never know, because they make no difference. The colour of a man's eyes, even if he's alive or dead."

"You mean Mr Conroy?"

"I meant Klauer. Dead now anyway, regardless of how things went. History doesn't care either way."

"Not necessarily."

Verrine looks pleased to have elicited some resistance. "Are you going to tell me about the butterfly effect? Tiny details changing the course of history? I don't believe that nonsense."

"You're a fatalist?"

"No, I believe we can all make a difference. I just don't waste my time on details."

"I'm guessing you don't play an instrument."

He laughs. "*Touché*. You're right, I could never have been a performer. But I've helped launch a few careers."

The waiter has reappeared, this time to replace redundant cutlery that had already been on the table when they arrived, with implements deemed appropriate to their order. Details, Paige thinks. Maybe Verrine's right, we waste too much time on ones that make no difference.

"I want to know more about the Klauer piece," Verrine says.

"You already know more than I do."

"But you've played some of it, you know how it sounds. What did David say about it?"

"Didn't he tell you?"

"I want to hear it from you." Verrine's look is momentarily steely, Paige can imagine him as boss of some big company, calmly firing an employee after years of faithful service, and again his eyes move to her breasts though this time they stay there a little longer. She doesn't dislike his attention, instead she feels herself drawing power from it, and almost without thinking, she flexes her back, a movement that swats his gaze like a fly.

"The Klauer's an interesting work," she says confidently.

"Romantic or modernist?"

"Hard to say."

"If it was a film soundtrack, what sort of film would it be?"

This is hard too; Paige thinks of the slow movement and tries to imagine the actors it would accompany, but all she can see is an empty landscape, remote forest or wetland, somewhere beautiful yet bleak. "Arty," she says.

"I was afraid you might say that. No chance of making that your concert debut, then."

"I already told you, I don't have the score."

"Oh yes, that's right," Verrine reminds himself. "But would you be able to play any of it from memory if you had to?"

"Why might I have to?"

"I was simply wondering."

Their meal arrives; the risotto is a little tit-shaped mound that looks like a starter. Fortunately Paige isn't hungry, Verrine's manner has somehow taken away her appetite. He slashes his bloody steak with enthusiasm. She says, "You mentioned on the phone about possibilities. Performances."

"That's right." He chews a piece of meat and looks as if he's thinking of her body.

"So how would that work?"

"One step at a time, Paige. First I'd like to find David so the three of us can discuss this together."

"Mrs White can give you an opinion."

"I'm not looking for a reference," he says with a voice that's suddenly cutting, effortlessly dismissive. "I want to know why you're pretending you haven't heard from him."

She feels the blood fall from her face. "What?"

His manner abruptly changes. "Only joking, Paige."

"Why would you think he'd contact me?"

"Because you're special."

Conroy's delusion: definite star quality. Paige says nothing.

"We've got to find him."

So none of this is about her after all; Verrine wants to get in touch with his act. "What if he's killed himself?" she says bluntly.

"He hasn't. I know David, the pattern's familiar. He's prone to paranoia, sometimes feels he needs to run away and hide. Conspiracies, threats, he suddenly sees them popping up everywhere and can't cope. Usually resurfaces after a few weeks but I can't wait that long."

"Look, Mr Verrine, I never had much to do with Mr Conroy, his mental health isn't my business. I'll be honest, I thought we were going to talk about my career, not his."

Verrine is barely listening, he summons the waiter with a wave of his hand and orders another glass of wine to replace the one he's drained. Then he says, "It's you I want to talk about, Paige. But you're wrong about David, closer to him than you realise. You're his new discovery, his little star, he shows you something incredibly precious, shares it with you, this lost work he wants you to learn, a secret he keeps even from his wife."

"I thought he didn't have one."

Verrine's smile is undented. "Joking again. So let's talk business. You're young, pretty and talented. That's a combination I like. But a career doesn't simply happen, it has to be made. First thing we want is an endorsement, David's won't do because to be perfectly frank his opinion no longer carries the weight it used to. I'm thinking maybe Paul Morrow."

"Send him a recording?"

"We set up a meeting and you play for him."

She can't believe this is real. "He'd honestly do that? Hear me play?"

"It's exactly how he started, Pogorelich heard him at Steinway Hall."

Paige can imagine it already, the instrument in front of her and Morrow just out of sight, can feel the pressure as she reaches for the keys. Her whole life resting on a single make-or-break performance, the verdict of one person.

"Well, Paige? Think you'd be up to it?"

"Mrs White would never let me."

Verrine laughs. "Your teacher? What's she got to do with it? It's David who'll be coaching you through this one, assuming we can find him. Though we won't tell him the plan, of course. You'll play for Morrow and if it's a thumbs up I can guarantee we'll be negotiating a recording contract within days. Better do something with your hair, though, and think about your wardrobe, I'm obviously no expert on that side of it but you've got a good figure, Paige, you should show it off. Bit of cleavage."

It's dizzying, this sudden vision of herself being wanted and admired. "Can I say anything about it to my parents?"

He shakes his head solemnly. "This is business, Paige, the big bad real world. Not a word to anyone, otherwise we risk blowing everything. What will you play for Morrow?"

"I suppose it would have to be Chopin."

"No way," Verrine says at once. "Forgive me, Paige, but to impress Paul Morrow with Chopin you'd need to be world class, and no matter how much David rates you, you're not in that league. We've got to be realistic, it's promise we're selling, not achievement. It's got to be a piece Morrow doesn't already know, in fact I'm thinking it should be a piece that nobody knows."

"Klauer?"

"Right on the money. So we drag David out of wherever he's sulking, make sure he hasn't turned the Klauer score into paper aeroplanes or roll-ups, get him to take you through it. You learn the whole thing, start to finish. When Morrow hears it, who knows, maybe a new star is born. Here's to a beautiful collaboration, Paige." He reaches across to shake her hand, the same firmness she registered at the start, only now the grip lasts longer, his palm is cool, she thinks hers must feel soft and wet. Then he gives her his card, elegantly printed and embossed, bearing what she assumes must be the name of the agency he works for.

"So there's only one small problem," Verrine adds as she puts the card away in her purse. "We need David. If he calls, as I'm sure he will, you know what to do. Arrange to meet him and tell me about it at once."

Paige leaves the restaurant feeling elated at the prospect of playing for Morrow, yet despondent that it all still hinges on Conroy. Verrine calls a couple of times over the following days but on each occasion Paige's report remains negative. She visits Morrow's website, gets to know the rugged face she may never meet, Googles Chopin and checks what Verrine said about his heart, his eyes, it all matches, meaning it's true, or that Verrine got his factoids from Wikipedia. The company name on his card turns out to be some kind of media conglomerate, the fancy site goes on about passion and mission without ever really specifying exactly what they do.

When Verrine next calls he tells her the meeting with Morrow is scheduled, still weeks away. He's a busy man, Paige sees the filled diary in her head, imagines the powerful feeling of being acclaimed but feels the balancing weight of failure and rejection: Morrow is as hypothetical and unreal as his website. Again she tells Verrine she hasn't heard from Conroy, and now his irritation shows. "We've got to find the fucker."

"If I can't get the score we'll need an alternative."

"There is no alternative," Verrine says witheringly. "Get it or the meeting's off."

"But…"

"We only get one shot, Paige, and it has to be done right. Klauer or nothing."

She can't understand why he's so adamant, there are plenty more unknown compositions in the world. Mrs White seems pleased with Paige's progress, but while playing the Scherzo in C sharp minor for her later that week, the picture in Paige's mind is of decomposing eyes, a rotting heart. During the customary break for tea and biscuits Paige asks with fake casualness about the issue that matters so much to her: has there been any news?

Mrs White nods. "He sent a resignation letter."

"Then he's all right."

"From what I hear, it wasn't the standard kind of resignation. Said he needed to stay hidden until he could defeat forces trying to destroy him. I'm not sure if he's getting any kind of psychiatric treatment but he clearly needs it."

"Does anyone know where he is?"

"I don't think so. But he got in touch and that might mean he's ready to look for help."

A whole week goes by with no word from Verrine, then she gets a call.

"Paige?"

"Mr Verrine, I…"

"This is David Conroy."

It's what she's been waiting for, though now that it's happening she feels no relief. She's been convincing herself that the audition with Morrow would be a waste of time, Conroy's sick and best avoided.

"Are you alone, Paige? Can anyone hear us?"

"I'm on the bus."

"Get off now, I'll call again in five minutes."

She's on her way to a doctor's appointment but does as he says, getting up in the swaying vehicle and alighting at the next stop, in a residential area she doesn't know. She waits on a quiet corner, long enough to consider how she'll handle it. When he rings back she asks at once, "Where are you?"

"I can't tell you, it's too dangerous. And don't try calling this number, it won't work."

"You should come back to the college."

"Everything's wrong, Paige. Don't you feel it? Didn't you notice? The needle jumped, everyone's mind was on something else."

This is what a nervous breakdown sounds like and it's not Paige's fault, has nothing to do with her, but he's trying to make her feel involved, and that's the trouble, she is. "People want to help you."

"I'm in the wrong life. None of this should be happening."

"We all have moments like that."

"Laura's gone."

"I know," she says, playing along with the fantasy. "She walked out on you."

He shouts, "The whole fucking world walked out!"

She waits silently until he calms down and apologises. All she wants is the score. "Are you at home?"

"I can't go back there."

"Then tell me where you're staying. Or perhaps we could meet." Immediately she realises this might sound too eager, she switches instead to flattery. "I preferred your lessons to Mrs White's. Wish I could have seen more of that Klauer work you gave me."

"Has anyone contacted you about it?"

"No."

At Conroy's end Paige can hear a sound she equates with thought, something like an indecisive sigh and the rubbing of his chin, while around her there's birdsong from empty gardens, an occasional passing car. Eventually he says, "We can't meet, it would be too much of a risk. The last thing I'd ever want would be for you to come to any harm."

"You wanted to perform the Klauer."

"It'll never happen"

"Then it's lost again?"

Another silence, she's sure he suspects nothing. Right now, Paige feels real pity for this weak man who's become fixated on her for no reason and is entirely the maker of his own misfortune. It's not her duty to feel sorry: she owes him nothing.

"Send it to me," she says, breaking into his hesitation.

"The score? But surely…"

"Mail it to me at the college. Nobody will know I have it. A perfect way to keep it safe. I really want to help you."

She hears him struggling to find words. "Paige…"

"Just send it."

"Guard it carefully. Tell no one. I know I can trust you."

1924

Capri

ONE-WAY STREET

Asja has gone into a shop to buy almonds but doesn't know
the Italian word; a German gentleman helps her with the
translation. Small round glasses; thick, dark hair; intellectual,
from a well-to-do background. And clumsy. He insists on
helping her with the packages but drops them, accompanying
her to the place where she's staying. His name is Walter
Benjamin. He's been here in Capri for some time, would she
mind if he were to call on her? Next day Asja cooks spaghetti;
he explains he's noticed her already some time before, walking
across the piazza. This is not how he falls in love with her.
This is how he announces the existence of a theoretical notion
willing to be made real. Love is the translation of concept into
action.

NO ENTRY

Benjamin has come to Capri to work on his habilitation thesis which will qualify him to teach in a university. He is to remain here for six months while his estranged wife and their young son stay in Frankfurt. Asja Lacis is a dark-eyed Latvian actress and theatre director who lives in Russia and has been a Bolshevik since before the Revolution seven years ago. She is staying on Capri with her partner and daughter. Benjamin tells her his thesis is on *Trauerspiel*, a style of Baroque drama characterised by violence and suffering. She asks him why anyone should waste time studying old plays that nobody reads.

POTEMKIN

The connection between a battleship and the many workers who hammered its rivets is like that of worshippers in regard to the idols of organised religion; the fetish-character of commodities leads to their being seen as phantoms whose assumed reality supersedes that of the people who made them. Thus our existence within capitalism is a condition of dreaming. Asja awakens him to this. He writes to friends about the interesting communist he has met, and with whom he is having long discussions. He sends postcards to his wife, telling her he is fine. Their relationship was extinguished some time ago; he feels closeness only towards his son, because Benjamin has not forgotten how to see the world with a child's eye of fear and wonder. He agrees with Baudelaire, childhood is the state closest to original sin, therefore purest. In the streets and brothels of Paris, Baudelaire stirred himself from dogmatic slumber, saw through the illusion, appreciated that modern life is an allegory whose signs can mean anything. Possessions, money, family, home: skeletons of their own contradiction.

VANITY MIRROR

Love begins with the contemplation of beauty, yet contemplation is a situation produced by capitalist production. Love itself is therefore allegorical: Asja could be anybody, she is the shape of the particular emptiness Walter brought with him to this Italian island, and it is the exactness of fit that bewitches him, the stencil of an unfulfilled desire waiting only to attach itself to a name. Asja: again and again he inscribes it, admiring the concordance between sound and image. I love you, he writes secretly to himself. I want to be with you, I want to leave my wife and child and live only with you. I want to be living the past that we will jointly remember, reading these words that will have become historical fact.

Capitalism is a mass narcosis whose ur-myth is the false promise: you can be happy. But love is this same dream, an internalised mythology, and Asja laughs at him: I am not a muse of the bourgeoisie, I am a proletarian and a free woman. I am not an unpaid prostitute who will be told whom I may or may not sleep with; I satisfy my physical needs and desires as I see fit. Free your own mind and heart, Walter, if your marriage is unhappy then get out of it.

–But what about our son?

He needs real love, not the illusion of an outmoded institution.

–How am I to find happiness?

Only through revolutionary action.

It is the Copernican turn of his heart; he came here to finish his thesis on Baroque drama but already he is thinking of another project: a book of fragments, epigrammatic or even surreal in character, apparent irrelevancies serving to create new, unintended meaning. And though he will go to Moscow, the centre of his thought will be Paris, the covered arcades where Baudelaire realised he was strolling in Hell.

Asja, I love you, he writes. I want to be able to look at your face every day; see how, like a mountain beside a lake, it changes with every passing cloud, every fluctuation of pressure and temperature. I want to see your breasts, kiss your belly and that catacomb, place of skulls, your lap where a new dream breaks all fetters and submerges us. I want to be human with you, mortal, slowly ruined by time until we are both dust together. I have never known this certainty of disaster.

–Walter, you are delightful and I so much enjoy being with you. I can think of no more stimulating companion, with your astute mental faculties, your understanding of philosophy. But you're clumsy, and things will fall.

CONSPIRACY

1. By all means discuss the book you are writing, but do not disclose its essence, any more than you would tell a child how a magic trick is done.

2. Make note of everything. For example, the conversation with the unusual Frenchman.

3. Adhere to the timetable of an honest worker. Writing is like engineering, done with the hands.

4. Think always of the one who is the cause of all this. Keep her image in mind, be faithful to it. Love every sentence as you love her. That is to say, without hope or expectation.

5. Difference between document and artwork: the former serves to educate the public, the latter discovers truth.

6. In every philosophical project there is an esoteric quality. Expect understanding no more than you crave applause.

7. Keep a favourite pen, a well-ordered desk, and dedicate yourself to making ideas surrender themselves to you – for

they alone will yield to your advances.

PLEASE USE ASHTRAYS
Walter Benjamin is sitting on the terrace of a café overlooking the bay. He knows several Germans staying on the island, and has been busying himself with excursions, social visits, letter writing, conversation. But today he is alone, with only his notebook and his thoughts. The thesis on *Trauerspiel* is finished; next will be his book of fragments, it will be called *One-Way Street*, and he will dedicate it to Asja.

A man comes and sits at another table, a foreigner like Benjamin, of similar age. They greet one another; the man responds in French, and after exchanging a few pleasant words they agree to sit together. Like Benjamin, the Frenchman has been on Capri for some time, has covered much of the same ground, both physically and socially, though neither claims any recollection of the other. They share a bottle of wine and a dish of olives; alcohol creates an air of friendship that might not otherwise have manifested itself so quickly.

Benjamin explains why he came here; he hopes to get a permanent position at Frankfurt University if his thesis is accepted.

"Is it a good thesis?"

"As good as I could make it, though perhaps that will be the problem, since success in circumscribed fields is dependent on adherence to existing categories of thought rather than the creation of new ones."

"You speak like a philosopher of art."

"And you, if I may say so, have the air of a poet."

The stranger laughs. "You mean an eccentric? I adopt certain local habits, my razor is not too sharp, I have no woman telling me how I should look."

"Did desire bring you here?"

"Only for knowledge, I study mathematics. Here is a problem for you, Epimenides the Cretan says that all Cretans are liars: do you believe him?"

"I know the paradox very well, there is something demonic in its circularity."

"It's a devil of a riddle, that's for sure. What about the barber who shaves every man who doesn't shave himself? Or the set of all sets that don't contain themselves?"

"Children's puzzles have always appealed to me, especially visual ones."

"To be consistent is to exist, that is the law of mathematics, a single violation should be enough to make the entire edifice vanish into non-being. Yet we live in an age of paradox, science has demonstrated it. Time can be slowed or quickened, space is curved, light is neither wave nor particle, or perhaps is both. There are our new categories of thought."

SHAKE BEFORE OPENING

The nineteenth century is when the crowd, the mass, becomes generally recognised as an object of history; it is in opposition to the crowd that the modern concept of the individual arises. Poe's story, 'The Man Of The Crowd', depicts the view through a coffee-house window: real life is what happens on the street, the interior is a place of illusion. The crowd is a reservoir of energy, a kaleidoscope equipped with consciousness, creating collision, surprise, chance. Gambling becomes a widespread and socially acceptable bourgeois pastime. The victors of revolution are the speculators. Marx says of Darwin's theory that it serves as a scientific basis for the class struggle, a death-blow to teleology, a rational-empirical explanation of historical progress; though without the inclusion of proletarian consciousness it is simply a description of capitalism itself. Baudelaire translates Poe's story, appreciating the revulsion inherent in it. Like Rousseau he reverts to solitary wandering, which is to say savagery. Urban industrialised life is dependent on fear of being alone, yet manufactures isolation. Love is a commodity whose inflated price we must recognise. Like any stock, its value exists only by virtue of shared belief.

GRADUS AD PARNASSUM

"I have made an extensive study of Boltzmann's thermodynamics," the Frenchman continues. "All of nature, it appears, is statistical."

"Nature itself, or our view of it?"

"Who knows? But since entropy rises inexorably, the universe must fade and decay."

"Then physics is a form of allegory."

The Frenchman slaps his thigh and exclaims with delight at this observation. "Yes, the allegory of chance, a cosmic casino. Are you a betting man?"

"I have insufficient love of money."

"Gambling is not about money, it is about perpetually renewed hope. Every turn of the wheel is independent of the previous one, the past is erased. Would you put a loaded revolver to your head?"

"Of course not."

"Then perhaps you have an insufficient love of life. I had a friend who was an incurable gambler, his lucky charm was a counterfeit coin made of glass."

"And what do you do?"

"For a while I was a musician with dreams of being a great composer. Now I am a philosopher like yourself."

"A natural consequence of disillusionment."

"Come to think of it, I believe I may have noticed you previously. Aren't you a friend of the Russian actress?"

HIGH VOLTAGE

Prostitution is described as the oldest profession because it is the prototype of wage labour in general. The worker comes to see time as a commodity he can sell, and capitalism becomes its perpetual degradation, an attempt to buy time at lowest cost. Time travel became a theme of fantastic fiction only after the invention of the motor car: it is the myth of instantaneous arrival, just as the whore is the myth of instantaneous gratification. The greatest good is attached to whatever can "save time", an acceleration imagined to preserve the moment of youth while hastening us towards death. In the modern allegory of commodities, the whore occupies a special position analogous to that of the skull in the Baroque.

REFRIGERATOR

Asja, you say you sleep with anyone you choose, that your partner doesn't mind and does the same, because this is the most progressive form of existence. But do you really choose freely? Is there a hidden mechanism of association, a shell trick that gives the illusion of will and makes us believe in the power of choice when actually the game is rigged so that one must always lose? The Frenchman, he's another, isn't he? You sleep with every man on this island except me, because I'm the only one who loves you.

Consider my position. I have a wife in Frankfurt, a child I love dearly and would never do anything to hurt. My wife is an outstanding person, morally and intellectually, I admire and respect her. Yet I don't desire her. Belief has abandoned me, as it abandoned the millions who saw their currency devalued to nothing. It is not only a wrecked economy that has brought me to Capri, it is also a wrecked marriage, one I know to be doomed, because it exists only on the plane of material reality, a surface without metaphysical depth. For a long time, thoughts of escape: to Palestine, Paris, anywhere.

I cannot resist this capitalist love, this desire to own and live in contemplation of you, to be loved by you. I envy the air that surrounds you, the light that reflects from your face when you waken, your eyes that are like an infinite ocean, I regret every minute of my life that has not been spent with you, all of it wasted. My life is not to be found in drawers, photographs, letters tied with ribbon, souvenirs without context; it lies in the future I yearn for. I will sacrifice everything for you, this is the meaning of passion, which is to say suffering and martyrdom, I shall be annihilated by your immortality, it is what I wish, though I know the desire is not a free one: that is what renders it authentic. We cannot choose whom we love; love chooses us, its emblem a skeleton wielding a scythe.

SEASON'S GREETINGS

"Yes," says Benjamin, "I know Miss Lacis. You're a friend?"

"I saw you with her," the Frenchman declares as a fly settles on the rim of Benjamin's wine glass. "You're in love with her, aren't you? I could tell. Don't think I'm being rude, I'm an eccentric, that's all, I speak my mind. We French, you understand, are experts in love."

"You already told me you're half-German."

He laughs. "German only in my head, thank God, but I have the heart of a Frenchman. Oh yes, I've loved, many times, and always truthfully, I'm no libertine. But you see, sir, I embrace risk, and what greater risk is there than love? The game is only worth it if the stakes are high, and that means you must first of all love life. What are the two things men kill themselves over? Money and women. I asked if you would put a loaded revolver to your head. I've done it. Pulled the trigger and... click. I live another day. Imagine if everyone in the world were to do that."

"Millions would die."

"And the rest would love life. They would end all war and poverty, live together in peace and prosperity in a world blessed by chance."

"You're a utopian."

"While you, I take it, are a Bolshevik, like the actress."

An unexpected challenge to define himself; Benjamin doesn't know what he is. "I think Marx was a philosopher of profound insight."

"But does the situation in Russia prove his theory? You can hardly call it a Marxist revolution, more like a Blanquist one."

"You mean a conspiracy rather than a proletarian uprising? Blanqui never had much success with that in France."

"But Lenin has in Russia. Make everyone think it's a popular revolution when really it's a coup: that's genius."

LINGERIE DEPARTMENT
Comparison between Baudelaire and Blanqui: their isolation. De Tocqueville saw Blanqui at his trial and described him as looking like a skeleton in an overcoat, a hideous apparition. Baudelaire drew a portrait of Blanqui, his idol. The connection may be arbitrary: all the more reason to look into it more deeply.

DO NOT LEAN OUT OF THE WINDOW
"We haven't even introduced ourselves, my name is Pierre Klauer."

"Walter Benjamin. And you must tell me exactly how you know Miss Lacis."

"Oh, I was invited to a dinner party a few weeks ago and she was among the guests. Then not long afterwards I noticed her with you."

Klauer must really have remembered it as soon as he arrived at the café and saw Benjamin sitting there. Nothing is random.

"You say you were a composer."

"I gave up music and haven't touched a piano in ten years."

"I find that extraordinary."

"Some men forego sex, I renounced music, which is easier for me."

"But why?"

"Because I no longer believed in it. Rather, I came to believe in something else. I was working on a large-scale orchestral piece, all I had done was a piano version; but that, I decided, would be my final work. As a composer I died. And was reborn."

"As what?"

"A man who loves life. But you, sir, you aren't happy, and it's because of the actress. She's leading you a merry dance, anyone can see it, even a perfect stranger like myself who happened upon you both in a restaurant."

"It was really so obvious?"

"Painfully so. Intellectuals are always the worst victims, too much thinking."

"Then what should I do?"

With a bent finger Klauer beckons his companion closer. "Get hold of a revolver, put a single bullet in it, spin the chamber and let fate decide."

He imagines Asja's face when she hears: Walter Benjamin has killed himself. He imagines his wife and son, his friends.

But mostly he imagines Asja.

"What if I survive?"

"That's the point, my friend, you will. Or if you don't, you'll never know anything about it, so what is there to lose?"

It is Pascal's wager for the era of mass production: the phantasmagoria of immortality.

"I lack your courage," says Benjamin. "And what of your family and friends, did you renounce them too?"

"Completely. Though I did return to my parents' home in Paris, just once. I knew they would be away, I only wanted to see the place."

"You doubted your decision to leave?"

"Not at all, I thought of retrieving my last work and burning it. And as I walked in those once-familiar rooms I truly felt myself to be a ghost, for my mother had made the place a shrine to my memory. Here is posterity, I said to myself, here is what you craved, to be remembered, and what does it amount to? The tears of those few who knew you, the continued indifference of the multitude who did not. Pierre Klauer can be removed from the world like a loose brick and who will notice the hole he leaves?"

"You say you loved women."

"They found other men. We are interchangeable."

"If everyone thought like you there would be no art or science, no great works passed down the generations."

"And every generation would be a world renewed. But I didn't burn my score, because when I opened the drawer of my desk I found that it was gone, in fact for a moment I wondered if it had ever really been there. Its destiny, you see, was always to be non-existent, and I was glad that it was missing, I hoped that someone else had put a match to it, as I would have done. Yet the drawer wasn't empty. I had also deposited a book there, that I used while composing the work."

"The source of your inspiration?"

Klauer smiles. "You could say that. I took it with me and still have it."

"Then you are more attached to art and literature than you care to admit."

"The book is neither," the Frenchman says with an air of satisfaction, as though a point has been scored. "It's very old, written in a language I don't understand, elegantly bound in yellow calfskin. And now that my finances have taken a bad turn I'm thinking of selling it. I expect I'll let it go for far less than it's worth."

"I'm a collector of books."

"Are you really? Then isn't this a fine stroke of chance for both of us?"

Chapter Seven

Conroy sits alone in the darkness of his rented flat, place where no one can find him, view through the uncurtained window of purple night clouds scummed with streetlight orange. In a world gone mad he's the only one who can see the truth. They made Laura disappear, now it's Conroy himself who must surely be next. Eliminate all witnesses, erase the evidence, already he can feel the breeze of annihilation airbrushing him out of history. That's why he's hiding, covering his tracks, making himself a non-person before those bastards can do it to him. If oblivion's the only option it'll be on his terms, not theirs.

Art and death: two lines of escape. And another, disappearance. The landlord wanted references, bank details. Conroy gave a false name and a wad of cash and that was sufficient, he's been here a week and no one has knocked on his door. A telephone squats in a corner on the grubby carpet, Conroy doesn't know if it's connected and doesn't plan on using it. His mobile went in a bin, his laptop is in the house he left.

Conroy refills his whisky glass, the bottle's nearly empty.

The portable TV is perched muted on a cardboard box he hasn't bothered to unpack, he can see the start of a science documentary, that physicist who used to be a pop star or something, kind everyone can relate to. He's standing on a mountain side waving his arms, Conroy thinks of turning the sound up but the remote is further away than the Glenfiddich. He couldn't bring a piano here, not even the upright, enforced musical celibacy is driving him nuts. This is what it's like, life without art. Wake up, do stuff, watch TV, go to sleep, start over next morning and you're no different except a day older.

Silent images of scientific authority: that big machine where they smash atoms. The space telescope. An urge to play but no instrument, his final greatest loss, and like all the others self-inflicted. He drove away his lover and his public, his recording label and his students, denied himself everything that was most precious, like he planned to screw up right from the start, planned his own destruction. Like Klauer. The dark demonic rhythm in his skull is the first movement of *The Secret Knowledge*, he hears its strident chords, feels left-hand leaps he'll never show to anyone. The performer needs an audience, take that away and it's God or nothing. Music is truth, the world prefers illusion.

The programme note still writes itself inside his head, critical commentary on an event that will never happen. There is no "secret knowledge", that surely is the implicit message of a work determined, like the man who made it, to shock. Striking is its quality of montage, the disconnectedness of components sequentially juxtaposed without evident logic. Like getting back from a concert tour and finding your partner has been unexisted. That sudden theme in G sharp minor: where else is it to be found, in the remaining composition or entire universe? Its singularity is guarantor of significance and critical death sentence. When complicity is the only possible success, failure becomes imperative. What Conroy's telling himself is that the sole available outcome of all this is disaster.

He needs to look up some references but hasn't brought his books; he tries to recall what Adorno said about the commodification of music. Mass culture replaces critical appreciation with mere recognition: to hear anything often enough is equivalent to liking it. We become nicotine addicts conditioned to think that what we crave is what we genuinely need and desire, the vocabulary of taste reduced to saying that a tune has a good beat. What the artist and philosopher have in common is their apprehension of a future existing unacknowledged within the present. Klauer could foresee the urban masses for whom the iPod would offer essential diversion.

He stretches for the remote and raises the sound, bringing the physicist's chummy northern vowels into audible focus. *Hundreds of millions of light years, and us a single tiny speck.* Computer graphics colourfully erupt, dazzling as a stained-glass window. It dawns on Conroy he's like the average person in one of his own concerts, nagged by desire for self-improvement but motivated more by hunger for distraction. When the TV physicist was a kid he must have been doing equations and reading textbooks same as Conroy was practising scales, not for fun but out of a rare unnameable compulsion that amounted to belief in the future.

Instead of a single universe there's a multiverse.

And then the phone rings. Takes a moment to recognise the sound that's startled him, insipid peeping from the corner with a dodgy stain where something maybe had a crap once, goes and lifts the receiver, plastic's an unnameable colour between beige and yellow, sticky in his stooping grip. Holds the dirty thing to his ear and waits, says nothing, expects a voice but there's only the sound of empty wires and lonely nights, some jerk like him hoping it's a woman at the other end, though against his own TV's low mumble Conroy can't even hear breathing, a void without background.

An infinite number of possible worlds and alternative realities.

The caller's holding, this is almost entertaining, Conroy walks back across the room, dragging the phone unit that dangles from the end of the handset cable like a wounded animal, lifts the remote from the chair arm and kills the volume, lets his attention fall fully on the absence at his ear, the black hole of non-being. A tease he won't give in to, the crackle of static is a symphony, a constellation of diamonds on a velvet cushion of silence, he rests his head against the softness of endless stars. The line goes dead.

They've got his number. He needs to move on, find another safe house, though he's so tired he wonders if it might be better to surrender. Slumped in the armchair once more he gazes at the television, prefers it without sound. Closes his eyes and when he opens them can't tell if he's seeing the programme or an advertisement, whatever it is he won't buy it. Closes again then suddenly it's morning, the sky white as bird-shit, mouth like sandpaper, limbs stiff and his head aching.

Later he's in the park, sitting on a bench spilling milk from a carton on his chin and overcoat while cold sunshine burns his eyes. He's thinking about Paige, whether to send the score like she asked.

"Hello, David."

Startled, Conroy turns to see beside him a haircut and zippered jacket he recognises. It's the police inspector.

"What do you want? Put another bug on me?"

"Those students, the ones your neighbour saw."

"I've done nothing wrong."

"Give me their names."

He has to protect Paige. "I never saw them."

"They were at your house. And you've been making abusive phone calls."

"I don't live there any more."

"Wishing our soldiers dead. Inciting violence. We have to think of public safety, national security."

"I'll give you any help you want as long as you tell me where Laura is."

"This was never about her."

Conroy drains the last of the milk and wipes his lip. "I've been trying to remember the assignment she was on."

"Let's stick to the point."

"Some big corporation."

"How many others were involved?"

"New technology. Does something to your brain."

"They posted those messages from your computer. You do realise you could go to prison for this, David? Unless you decide to co-operate."

The reality is startling; Conroy looks at the inspector's profile beside him and sees a man confident of his own power, a man like a particle accelerator. "What messages?"

"Don't pretend you don't know. I'll give you time to think about it, but not long."

"Why not arrest me now?"

"Give us what we want and I'll make sure you get the help you need." The inspector stands. "Do the right thing." He walks away.

Conroy places the empty milk carton on the bench beside him, reaches into his pocket and searches until his fingertips find what he expects, the device that he pulls out, gleaming in the sunshine. He hurls it away across the grass and it makes his head feel clearer, there'd been a buzzing before but no longer, he can hear birdsong. In the distance, near some trees, a man stands watching him.

He doesn't know anything about those messages but needs to find out, he leaves the park swiftly, trying to lose the guy who's tailing him, though as he nears the library he sees him again, a figure on the opposite street corner facing the other way in a poor attempt at concealment. Inside the library Conroy finds a row of unused computers, he's never been before and expects to be able to log on freely but when he sits down at one of the screens he finds it prompting him to enter a number. Types a few random sequences but nothing works, then a woman with a false name badge interferes, says he can have temporary access if he shows proof of identity. He leaves immediately.

Outside there are closed-circuit cameras disguised as lighting fixtures. If our every movement is monitored and recorded then how can there possibly be time for anyone to watch it all? The accumulated information is greater than life itself, a paradox that follows him to the high street and an electronics store where he jabs at the keyboard of a display laptop and is again required to enter a password which a looming gangly assistant quickly supplies, leaning past Conroy to type, his nylon shirt exuding cheap deodorant. The assistant wants to know what sort of machine Conroy is looking for, whether it's for gaming or general surfing, for individual or family use, wants to know everything except who Conroy is, so Conroy says he'd like to try the internet for a few minutes and is left alone to play.

Only way the policeman could have connected those

seditious messages with Conroy was if his name was on them. So he searches for himself, just like he did with Laura, and the result is the same. He isn't there. A thousand near-matches, namesakes from all around the world: dentists, lawyers, accountants advertising their existence and expertise, but the pianist is gone, wiped like his lover. Conroy hurriedly extinguishes the page as the assistant returns, tells him he'll think about it, but what he's really considering is his own non-being, the impossibility of proving innocence when all evidence of supposed guilt has been removed.

He returns to his flat, only a matter of time before they come for him there. Climbing the bare common staircase that smells of piss and cider he reaches his front door, dented by pursuers of a former resident. The lock feels loose when he turns the key, as though someone might have tampered with it. Stepping inside he immediately senses another presence, and in the living room he finds it. On the battered sofa sits an elderly lady.

"Hello, dear," she says.

"Who the fuck are you?"

"My Pixie can't keep herself out of mischief, always roaming about."

"Your cat?" Conroy drops onto the armchair and looks at the genial silver-haired woman in her pale blue cardigan and large-beaded necklace. "How did you get in?"

She smiles. "You left the door wide open, I suppose Pixie came to inspect."

What's he supposed to do, offer her tea? "Where's Pixie now?"

"Gone back upstairs, I expect," the lady says unconcernedly, then from the pocket of her cardigan she takes a pack of playing cards, larger than normal so that at first he doesn't recognise what they are. She fans and holds them out in her tremorous hand. "Take one."

"What the hell is this?"

"Go on."

He does as she says, slides out a card and looks at it. The picture is like an old woodcut, hand-coloured, with the word *Pyramide* printed elegantly beneath a picture of an Egyptian monument.

"Show me what you picked."

He turns it towards her. "Are you going to tell my fortune?"

"It signifies wisdom."

"Who are you? This is about those students, isn't it?"

"Ancient knowledge, a great secret." She holds out the pack again so that he can choose another card. It shows a naked man and woman, Adam and Eve, with the inscription *Jardin*.

"A couple, a meeting," the lady explains. "Perhaps a fall."

Next he must take two cards, he consents with increasing bemusement but that changes instantly when he sees what they are. A pair of figures in mediaeval costume; one a stonemason, the other a glass-blower. The titles are *Pierre* and *Verrier*.

"Who put you up to this?"

"Stone denotes strength and fortitude, glass stands for great prospects or an auspicious discovery."

"Where did you get these cards?"

"I suppose I should go and see what Pixie's up to now…"

"How do you know about the secret knowledge?"

"Oh, I don't know any more about it than you do, dear."

She passes him the rest of the pack and Conroy begins to look through the cards. From their condition they seem recently made though the style of illustration is archaic; he supposes them to be a sort of tarot deck. One card shows a simple leather shoe and is called *Oeillet*, another that attracts

Conroy's attention has a rose bush in full bloom; he gazes at the blood-coloured flowers and a memory stirs in his mind.

"Rosier."

"Usually it means faith and purity."

"The people Laura was investigating."

"I'd really better go and see what that little rascal of mine's up to, would you like to keep the cards a while longer?"

Conroy nods silently, dumbstruck by revelation, while the lady tries to raise herself from the sagging sofa, making the effort several times until Conroy notices and reaches to help lift her, then she totters away, muttering to herself about the cat. Conroy hears the front door close and stares at the cards piled in his hand. The Rosier Corporation, that was what Laura called it. He needs to find out more but if he leaves again he's sure to be spotted by the man who's been following him, too risky even going to the window to check. So Conroy waits, immobile like an insect beneath a stone, watching the slow change of daylight and feeling the empty hours push shadows slowly across the walls of the room.

Must have fallen asleep because now it's dark, his body wooden like the old lady's, wrecked and invisible. The cards are gone, they aren't in his hand or lap or on the floor at his feet, as if she came back for them. He strains upright, sways with sleep still clinging to him, the sky outside livid again with night colour, purple and orange. He goes and looks down from the window and no one's there, they've given up. Safe to go out and find food.

Half an hour later he's walking in drizzle eating chips by the handful, throws the half-full container in a skip. Two women are having a drunken argument in front of a kebab shop, it stands next to the pallid glow of a place calling itself an internet café, white-walled room where a couple of foreign-looking youths sit staring at screens as a refuge from boredom. Conroy goes inside, buys a coffee from the machine, takes a seat and pays the access fee. The police can easily find him here but he doesn't care.

"Hey, darling." It's one of the women, standing unsteadily in the doorway and leaning on its frame for support, tits palely bulging like old lard. His stare unnerves her, a reminder of the state they've both let themselves fall into, though it doesn't sink in at first, instead she simply looks puzzled. Conroy imagines the scene if she was beautiful and sober, he anything but a loser, imagines it so clearly that he feels transfigured, wants to tell her about his secret mission, take her on the run with him. Instead he stares until she sneers back at him, "Fuck off," and waddles out of sight.

He wants to find out more about Rosier, begins typing but is soon interrupted.

"David?"

Must have been standing silently behind Conroy for some time. Dark jacket and tie, shirt a deep shade of burgundy, immaculately trimmed hair, olive skin. A neat, theatrical appearance like a stage hypnotist.

"You've been following me."

No one else in the internet café, the two slouching youths have left while Conroy was staring at the screen. There's only himself and the guy.

"Who are you?"

"Call me H."

"Are you with the police? The Corporation?"

H says nothing, draws up a chair, the only sound the whirring of computer fans and a distant siren outside.

"You've come to erase me, same as you did to Laura."

"You shouldn't have stopped taking your medication."

"That's not how this started."

H nods thoughtfully. "Who can say where anything begins or ends?" He reaches into his jacket pocket, brings out a fine silver chain, holds one end and lets it hang for Conroy's inspection.

"Laura's."

"Something I found." H twirls it in his fingers. "Where's the first link? Top, bottom, somewhere in the middle? Is what happens today caused by whatever occurred yesterday; or might events be explained by something still to come? You're a musician, you understand how everything leads to a final chord, a cadence, perhaps a resolution."

Conroy looks round towards the door and sees only darkness and emptiness beyond, as if the city itself has been obliterated. "You're not real. None of this is real."

"For example, think of some of your favourite piano compositions. Where does *Kreisleriana* end? Not the final note, that's for certain, it's still playing inside your head. Or the 'Ḥammerklavier' Sonata? Beethoven finished the whole thing and sent it to the publisher, then at the very last moment he decided to add a single bar at the opening of the slow movement. We hear it in the middle when really it's the conclusion – or beginning."

"What happened to Laura?"

"She never existed."

"Then why do I remember?"

"Mistakes happen." H smiles, crumples the thin chain in his fist and returns it to his pocket. "What if Beethoven's letter hadn't arrived at the publisher's in time, and the extra bar wasn't added? Would anyone notice? If things had gone a little differently, might we now rate Spohr over Schubert, or Hummel over Mendelssohn? If history could be altered…"

"It can't."

"Think of any piece you play: a fixed score, yet every performance is unique. Physical reality is like the score, existing outside of time. History is performance." H reaches again into his pocket and brings out something else that Conroy recognises.

"The old lady's cards. You broke in and took them."

H shuffles the deck without comment, then fans them, just as the lady did, and holds them out, face-down, for Conroy to make his selection.

"Why should I play this game, you've already made the choice for me."

H appears amused, even pleased. "A performer knows all about the tricks of persuasion. Yes, the game was rigged, you were always meant to lose, but go on, take a card, see what you get."

Conroy places his finger on one then immediately changes his mind and touches another.

"Are you sure?" H asks.

Conroy opts for a third, pulls the card from the man's grip and turns it to see the picture. A corpse dangling in a gibbet. "Suicide," he murmurs, reading the legend.

"What Klauer did and didn't do. The thing every artist yearns for."

"Death?"

H shakes his head. "Immortality. Forever sacrificing yourself, yet surviving."

"This was always about Klauer."

"It's about what he stole."

1967

West Germany

Theodor Adorno wakes, rolls and sees Ulrike still asleep beside him, pale shoulder studded with fine freckles. Late afternoon sunshine filters through the thin curtains of her apartment, it's in one of Frankfurt's noisier suburbs, swelled by immigrants and perpetually permeated, it seems, by amplified music. Teddie must be home before seven.

Praxis is the ensemble of means for minimising material necessity. It therefore becomes identical with pleasure. Yet pleasure is denied within a society that asserts only rational practicality. Being married and sixty-four years old shouldn't stop a man fucking his student. Ulrike appreciates the hermetic character of play. Her record collection includes only the latest rock-and-roll releases, nevertheless her non-compulsory attendance at his course on advanced dialectics has indicated to him acute awareness of the fundamental contradiction those commodities represent. Sex, too, can be understood negatively. That he is not with his wife should not imply infidelity. He has never kept secrets from Gretel, except when too nugatory to be worth mentioning.

Lying with her back to him, Ulrike's short brown hair leaves naked and exposed the vertebrae of her neck. Teddie traces the undulating ridge with his finger, she stirs and sighs, suddenly conscious of comfort, warmth, intrusion.

"I have to go," he says.

"Mmm."

She doesn't turn; her acceptance, which is rejection, disappoints him. Instead of leaving the bed as he ought, he gazes at the ceiling, noting its hairline cracks and peeling paint. One day Ulrike will be a philosophy lecturer, as he is now. At least that's the dream, though he doubts she's up to it.

She becomes fully awake. "Want some coffee?" she asks, sitting up and reaching for her cigarettes and lighter. Teddie doesn't care either way. He answers a different question.

"Tomorrow would have been Walter Benjamin's seventy-fifth birthday." Even as he says it, the future conditional evokes an inescapable antinomy. "There's a symposium at the university."

"I know."

"Will you come?"

"Do you want me to?"

"I'm to be the main speaker."

"Will Gretel be there?"

"It doesn't matter. I don't think so."

Ulrike breathes blue smoke into the static air. "Sure, I'll come."

Just how little truth converges with subjective idea, with intention, is evident to the most rudimentary consideration. Benjamin's dictum – the paradox of beauty is that it appears – is less enigmatic than it sounds.

"What'll you say?" she asks.

"Obviously I won't offer an *hommage* or appreciation. That would be vulgar."

She gets up, standing thin and naked in thought beside the bed. Her breasts are small, there is something almost emaciated about her appearance, yet youthful, defiant. She could be contemplating her own execution. She picks up some underwear, pulls a shirt over her head, begins to walk away. "What if there's another protest?" She peeks through the curtains at whatever isn't happening in the void outside.

"I'm sure there won't be."

"The movement's gaining support."

"Its motives are compromised."

At a recent seminar a group of students came and stood in front of the lectern, completely blocking Adorno's view of the audience. One of them read a series of pledges and demands ranging from solidarity with the people of Vietnam to complaints about the university cafeteria, then there was an open discussion about the meaning of political action in which Adorno took no part.

"They won't disrupt the symposium," he says. "Not given the sort of saintly figure Benjamin has become."

She turns. "You sound almost jealous."

Ulrike's swinging rump departs to the kitchen while Teddie remains prostrate, wondering if there will be coffee or even further sex before he goes. Of course he isn't jealous. His position in the Institute makes him custodian of the Benjamin archive, while his work on the same questions his late friend confronted, his duty to correct error, becomes easily equated in some minds with the false notion of legacy. All that is least essential in a philosopher can be summarised under the heading "biography". Hence the snide attacks and mischief-making of people like Arendt. What matters to them is not truth-content, but the preservation of a dead man's every sacred word, even the wrong ones. That is touching but misguided. Were Walter Benjamin alive today, thinks Teddie, he would have destroyed and rewritten a large proportion of the texts for which he is celebrated. He would have cared little for the birthday festivities planned in his honour.

He hears the water hiss and begin to boil. He knows he has never been handsome or attractive in the reified sense of movie actors; but there will always be discerning women for whom a discourse on Hegel is more seductive than a bunch of flowers. Ulrike is able to see beneath the social superstructure; he has taught her how. She comes back holding a striped mug in her hand. "I've never thought to ask you, Teddie. When's your birthday?"

"September eleven."

She sips, pauses. "That's a long way off."

"You don't think we'll be together then?"

"I mean, it's still only July."

No coffee, no sex. When Teddie gets home he finds his wife has already left for the theatre alone. He needs to prepare for the symposium. He should like to say something about Benjamin's position on Heidegger; Teddie has discussed his own in his most recent book, *Negative Dialectics*. The first edition has already sold out, a new one is being printed. Everyone has an opinion about it, even if they don't understand it, which is the majority position. Adorno is accused of obscurity, jargon-mongering, the very things he opposes. When the world is discussed in the clearest possible terms it becomes infinitely opaque. Are there existing things that cannot be considered concepts? A clear enough question, surely. That phoney Heidegger merely ontologises the pre-existing; Walter saw clearly enough the fascism already implicit in Heidegger's return to the mythological.

Not enough, though, to expound on negative dialectics, even given the level of public interest, not after recent events, the student shot by riot police. Adorno made his lecture class stand for a minute's silence in honour of the victim. One could call it a sentimental and therefore anti-philosophical gesture, like the Benjamin symposium with its tang of hero-worship, but the point was to recognise the significance of the present, not dwell on an invented past. Some of the students are speaking of a revolutionary moment, they say the Federal Republic is a fascist state, utter nonsense. They condemn a country where there are free elections and praise Mao for terrorising his own people. Their condition is despair, like Walter's, but also, fatally, it is disillusion.

He should address the question they keep asking him. At one of his lectures a girl came and handed him a teddy bear, simply trying to embarrass him, and said to the audience, how is critical theory to become critical practice? Some applauded, others jeered, but the question dogs him. He is a thinker, a theoretician, but what the youth of today demand is action, any sort of action. Class struggle is a mythology that lies conveniently within their grasp. By asking people to think, he becomes identified with the forces of oppression.

He has been accused of suppressing or distorting Benjamin's work because Benjamin was insufficiently Marxist, or else too much of a Marxist. His frantic and ultimately doomed efforts to give Benjamin research money and get him out of Europe are portrayed as manipulation, the arbitrary exertion of power. He has been a selective and partisan editor of their published correspondence. Let's be honest about all this. If Benjamin had not killed himself then he would not be on the pedestal posterity has made for him. He's like Anne Frank, a symbol that becomes a substitute for thought, a point of adhesion for pre-existing emotion. What of the forgotten? What of those denied even the status of concept?

He's beginning to feel his age. Two tasks lie before him: his aesthetic theory, which he expects to be his most lasting work, and his book on Beethoven. Perhaps he should talk about one of those. As long as some bearded hippie doesn't intervene.

He's already asleep when Gretel gets back, doesn't see her until next morning. Of course she'll be coming to the symposium; how could she miss such an important event? She loved Walter too. But she hasn't heard anything about the programme, nor can Teddie enlighten her. He understands it's a university event, but the organisation of it has been ramshackle, he's not even sure if it's intended for academics or the general public. Somebody noticed the anniversary, that's all. Felt it should be marked. Adorno's publisher is possibly involved. Perhaps the entire thing is a marketing exercise.

It takes place that night; Adorno shows up and among the audience in the large, well-filled auditorium he sees at least three women with whom he has been romantically involved, a few others with whom he'd like to be. He's expecting to give a lecture but the stage has a row of chairs behind a long table, microphones for half a dozen participants. Nobody bothered to tell him anything, explain what was wanted. There are many faces he doesn't recognise, faces who appear not to recognise him.

A young fellow comes and shakes him by the hand,

introduces himself as chairman for the evening, journalist on one of the left-wing newspapers. Can't be any older than thirty, thinning hair and thick-rimmed glasses, an earnest demeanour that gives him the air of someone in fancy dress. Other participants materialise; a lecturer Adorno knows, a writer, a woman who's apparently a film-maker, people from the margins of Frankfurt's intelligentsia. Such eclecticism mirrors only the most unfortunate aspect of Benjamin's endeavour. Adorno foresees a talk on Benjamin's use of hashish.

Eventually it gets going; they all have ten minutes to make whatever claim they can on the public's attention. The film-maker is planning a work based on Benjamin's life; this is the first that Adorno has heard of the project, which strikes him as tasteless and banal, the epitome of everything to which Benjamin stood in opposition. The lecturer then uses his ration of time to speak about the student protests and police violence, asking what Benjamin would have thought of it and reaching no conclusion more illuminating than that Walter would have been as upset about it as everyone else in the room. He was, that is to say, one of us, an emblem like those Baroque images he discussed so penetratingly, whose captions can signify anything we want them to.

The writer's offering is strangest and most outrageous of all: a story about Walter, a fictional depiction of the man Adorno knew personally, as though he were some legendary hero. This, thinks Adorno, is the limit point of historical sentimentalism; his gorge is rising even before he hears the first words of the story, the introduction is bad enough. Benjamin, the writer explains, was fascinated by the figure of Louis-Auguste Blanqui, and his theory that there are other worlds like our own, but with altered histories. Sheer nonsense, Adorno mutters to himself, barely concealing his words; Benjamin's interest was a small and characteristically eccentric part of a far larger analysis of the conditions of nineteenth-century capitalism. And so, the writer continues, in a way that is I hope faithful to Benjamin's insights, I have imagined how it might have been otherwise, if Benjamin had not died while fleeing from the Gestapo, but had instead escaped.

Adorno pushes back his seat, about to leave. The chairman stares at him, alarmed, and waves him to remain, a gesture that is both a request and a command. Adorno manages not to listen to the story, its inconsequentiality rendering it surprisingly easy to ignore, instead he looks at Ulrike, remembers her naked body when they made love, remembers every sound she made, and thinks how futile life is. In everything we do there is an element of exchange, and contemporary social relations, he reflects, are becoming subject to a devaluation far greater than what befell the Reichsmark nearly half a century ago. The result is a lapse into authoritarianism.

People are applauding that stupid story. Now at last it's Teddie's turn. He leans forward into the welcoming ambit of the microphone. "I knew Walter Benjamin," he says. "More importantly, I have spent decades studying problems that engaged his thought. A man's ideas, if they are at all original, are the property of no one, not even the man himself. To consider them such would be to deny them the autonomy that is their claim to significance. My intervention in Benjamin's ideas has been criticised in some quarters. This, however, is the practice to which critical theory naturally gives rise. Benjamin, who was a gifted linguist, once wrote of the task of the literary translator, saying it was not to make the translated work appear as if it were not a translation, but rather to make the work appear what it is, foreign, the product of a different culture. And everything we read is a kind of translation. Everywhere is a foreign country. I lived for some years in America, and all the time there I considered myself a European. Here in Europe, I feel at times as if perhaps I have become an American."

There is a shout from the audience, Adorno cannot hear the words but a moment later a person in another part stands up and begins shouting back. Two activists from opposing factions are having an argument. People tell them to sit down, order is restored though it is a false and uneasy order. He looks at Ulrike again but her attention is on the demonstrators. It is his wife Gretel who gazes lovingly at him, convinced as always by every word he says.

"Walter Benjamin's intention was to join me and my colleagues in America. An imaginative novelist might speculate on the ensuing biographical events, but who could envisage the philosophical insights that would have resulted, except for a philosopher? There we see the limitation of fiction in relation to philosophy, for fiction deals with the particular, the accidental, the psychologically arresting; whereas philosophy, while traditionally it encompassed only the most abstract and conceptual, nevertheless, in Benjamin's view and in my own, ought also to account for the particular, the unique, the never to be repeated or replicated. Then philosophy would finally have conquered fiction, and for the latter there would be no need. Why, we may ask, did Walter Benjamin, that most exquisite of prose writers and most discerning of critics, never write a novel, nor attempt one? It was because of this realisation he had, that a fully formed materialist conception of history would render fiction obsolete, like the magic-lantern shows he wrote about, which have been replaced by the distractions of cinema. Philosophy is truth, not fiction. And the truth is that Walter was a melancholy man as well as a genius. The truth is that even if the Gestapo had not pursued him, he would probably have killed himself in the end, if not in Spain then in some hotel room in New York, upset over yet another unrequited love affair. Was it his destiny? No, it was his predisposition. So forgive me, ladies and gentlemen, if I express my displeasure at the ease with which this man whom I knew has become an intellectual commodity."

An activist gets to his feet and this time his words are clearly heard. "You deny freedom and are a fascist."

Adorno answers calmly. "I deny the legitimacy of authoritarianism masquerading as free speech."

But there are more shouts, drowning him out, and then, as if a pre-rehearsed moment in the proceedings has finally been reached, three young women bring out a banner made of pieces of paper or card taped together, painted with bright green letters that say something not entirely legible about workers of the world. The girls shuffle out of their row in the audience and bring the banner to the front, accidentally tearing it on the way, then when they reach the stage, completely unopposed, they discard the remains of the banner and two of them sing while the third begins removing her clothes. At this point the celebration of Walter Benjamin's seventy-fifth birthday reaches its end.

Adorno is in his office at the university next day when he gets a phone call. The woman says her name but he doesn't catch it; he assumes it's one of the protesters and considers putting the receiver down; but no, she isn't phoning to apologise or launch a further attack, she had nothing to do with the demonstration; in fact, she says with an embarrassed laugh when he questions her, she's an elderly and, she likes to think, perfectly respectable lady. She simply wants to meet and discuss with him a matter concerning Walter Benjamin. This afternoon, perhaps?

She proposes a park; the weather recommends it, though there is also an air of mystery to the assignation. Is the conversation to be of a kind she would prefer no one to overhear? Parks, in Adorno's mind, are a place for clandestine lovers wishing to proclaim an illusory freedom. The woman says she's elderly but that could still signify fewer years than his own. Her voice is beautiful.

He arrives early and waits on a bench. Some sort of bird is hopping on the grass, he doesn't know the name. Sunlight perforates the trees, momentarily dazzles him, connects him with primal warmth. He remembers hearing it claimed that the sun emits radio waves.

Then he sees her, approaching slowly. Yes, he thinks, it's surely her, incongruous by her dignity, a moving statue, relic of an earlier time, perhaps a decade older than himself, yet straight-backed and without a walking stick. And yes, she's beautiful. He rises to greet her; she extends her slender hand.

"I am Yvette Carreau."

He finds himself making a bow, crooking his arm for her to hold. An old, extinguished world has come alive.

"My late husband was a collector," she explains as they begin walking, for she says she would prefer it, and he hears a trace of a French accent that hadn't been apparent on the telephone.

"A collector of what?"

"Miscellaneous objects and distractions. Also something of a gambler, willing to part with large amounts of money for items that might prove worthless. And a hunter, determined to catch the quarry he sought." She stops and turns to look at Adorno. "He met your friend Walter Benjamin on the night before he died."

Now Teddie understands. This woman has no interest

in him, only in the past he represents, the connection with history. She wants to tell him an anecdote he can put in a book or lecture. "Were Benjamin and your late husband intimately acquainted?"

"They met on only that single occasion. Some people say once is as good as never, but I've always felt that a single meeting can mean more than a thousand."

"An interesting observation. So your husband was in Portbou?"

"And I was with him, at the Hotel de Francia. Louis had the visas and Benjamin had what Louis wanted in return."

"My God."

"You see now why I wanted to meet."

"You could have told me this long ago."

"Not while Louis was alive. My late husband insisted there was a plot against my life, a secret cabal, from which he alone could protect me." They're reaching a boating pond; now Yvette would like to sit and watch the glittering water broken only by paddling ducks and the empty boats moored and rocking at the edge. They position themselves at a respectful distance from one another on the bench she selects. "Louis was a good and loyal husband. But he never believed that I really loved him, I see that now."

Adorno gives a cough of embarrassment. "What went wrong with the visas? Did Benjamin not have enough money for them?"

Yvette shakes her head. "All I know is what Louis told me, which is that Benjamin had somehow, quite unwittingly, acquired a book containing crucial evidence of the conspiracy. Louis wanted it in exchange for the visas he'd procured at great risk. And so I sat in the restaurant of the hotel while Louis went upstairs to see Benjamin, who had been arrested with some other Jews. A gramophone played nearby, it was a balmy evening and in different circumstances it could all have been romantic and pleasurable, yet I was tired, depressed, fearful. And when Louis came back he told me that he had the book, its former owner had the travel documents. We returned to our own hotel and next day back across the border to France. It was only much later that I learned the poor refugee had been a scholar of some importance, and that instead of trying to use the visas he had decided to take his own life."

Adorno is sceptical. "What was the book?"

She smiles. "Long ago I was engaged to a musician named Pierre Klauer. Fate stole him from me, but I was left with the key to his desk, where he said his latest work was to be found. It was Louis who retrieved it, a piano score ominously titled *The Secret Knowledge*. And how I treasured that relic of my sweetheart. So many times I wept over it, clutching it until the pages became bent and faded, but determined that it should live forever. Louis' acquisition of the work, right from under the noses of Pierre's parents, was the first indication to me, both of his ingenuity, and of the threat we jointly faced. Pierre's death was the work of an underground sect; I risked being their next victim. The music, Louis explained, was a coded message, the protocols of the organisation, but it lacked one vital thing. Pierre gave me the key to his desk, but not the key to the code. This was what had somehow fallen into the hands of Walter Benjamin, a book the society was determined to recover, at whatever cost."

Adorno glances at his watch. "This is most... unusual."

"I see that you are doubtful of my story. And you are right to be – for it was built on a lie. Louis always kept from me the secret knowledge that he said could only harm me, but when he passed away I felt as though my own life were no longer worth living. Come now, damned conspirators, I said to myself. Come and kill me, but before I die I shall unlock the code, break the spell of fear itself. I knew where the book was kept, knew the combination of the safe. Louis had forbidden me from opening it and I had obeyed, but now what else was I to do? So I brought it out into the light of the day, the slender volume that Walter Benjamin thought could save his life, as well as other papers stored with it. I sat at Louis' desk and looked at those cursed documents. And I realised at once: I had been deceived."

"What did you see?"

"First the book, written in some unknown language and peppered with symbols, hieroglyphs; it was no cipher but was itself in code. Why had this confused jumble been kept hidden from me? What might I have learned from it? Only that it was meaningless. But more than the book, it was the other papers that drew my attention, for what I had before me were notes for Pierre's work, sketches and drafts. Surely my husband must have retrieved these from the composer's desk along with the score, for a moment this was what I thought. But the pages told a different story. Mingled with musical notation there were verbal comments, suggestions, mathematical equations. The handwriting was not Pierre's. I even retrieved the letters I still kept from him, in order to verify what was so immediately obvious to me."

"He could have worked with an assistant."

"No, professor, there was no assistant. Because you see, I recognised the handwriting at once. I told myself it couldn't be true, yet there was no other explanation. The man who wrote those words was my husband. Certainly there was another hand at work in the drafts, another style of writing, but when I examined it all closely, so very closely, I understood what had gone on. As well as Pierre's letters I revisited the most sacred item of all, the score. And like a detective, with a magnifying glass in my hand, I discovered what I knew must be the truth. The work was a forgery. My husband, Louis Carreau, cobbled it together as a way of winning me for himself. He said he knew Pierre, this much I believe is true, and he must have seen his writing, practised until he was able to replicate it, penned what looks like an entire piece of music and claimed to have taken it from Pierre's desk. Made me hide it, so that in all the years I never heard it. I expect it would be only crude noise. Poor Louis had no ear for music."

"Surely you must hate him for it."

"I pity him. He saved me from my misery after Pierre died, but that was not enough, instead he felt the need to invent some other kind of salvation, more tangible and persuasive, that would bind us together. A great hoax reinforced by so many strange incidents over the decades, obscure items he acquired. And I never suspected a thing, because from the very start, Louis had done what would make his story most convincing, he had created the essential piece of material evidence that would extinguish all doubt. Some women lose a husband and discover he had another wife and home, another life, making a mockery of the love they claimed to feel. But when I discovered how I'd been deceived, it had the opposite effect. He did it all for me, because he thought he had to. He simply couldn't believe that I might love him only for what he was, for the good and pure heart that he had. How I miss the years of happiness we might have shared."

Adorno imagines the aftermath of his own death, Gretel reading every letter, recognising every name, being surprised by nothing. "Your story is a tragic one."

"The word is overused. They say your friend Benjamin was

tragic; others might call his demise typical."

"He made a fatal error."

"He was a fool, like Louis."

Adorno finds it a wise and admirable comment, but also deduces that the woman's late husband was not wholly wrong in doubting the possibility of love. "I thank you for this interesting piece of history, now I ought to return to my work." He begins to rise, Yvette holds his arm.

"I admit my story is bizarre and you had no need to hear it. But I wanted to speak of Walter Benjamin. The book he gave my husband is real."

"You thought it nonsense."

"Whatever it is, wherever it came from, even when we discard my husband's deceptions, it remains the fact that your friend carried the book over the Pyrenees; for him it was equivalent to life itself. I should like you to have it. To me it means nothing."

"And to me it should mean more?"

Yvette looks sadly at the bright water of the pond. "If you will not receive what I am offering then I shall destroy it. I suppose it has no place in the archive of Benjamin's papers, but perhaps he might have liked you to have what cost him so much effort."

Adorno considers the strange proposal; a gift that focuses with startling clarity the nullity of all gifts, their purely symbolic value, where what is symbolised is always an exchange, because the gift has to be accepted as well as given. This poor woman's life has been an illusion, her marriage a sham, her love affairs counterfeit. His acceptance would amount to telling her: it has not been wasted.

"Send it to me," he says, giving her his card. Then he bids farewell to Yvette Carreau, leaving her sitting on the bench where she watches the ducks, looking now like the old woman she always was. He walks away and forgets her. Already he's late for an encounter with Ulrike at her apartment.

The package arrives at his home the following day. Wrapped in brown paper he finds the slim, elegantly bound volume the Frenchwoman described; also some Xeroxed pages of musical manuscript and an accompanying note explaining them to be the work she spoke of. She knows it to be a fake, she writes, yet still cannot part with the original that has been her trusted companion for so many years.

Adorno leafs through the book, whose age and provenance only a specialist could determine. It is, as she said, written in some form of invented language, incorporating tables, diagrams and symbols one could guess to be mathematical or magical (categories indistinguishable except to the initiated). A frequently recurring mark resembling the Greek letter *psi* could equally be a pitchfork; Adorno suspects the work to be a coded treatise on demonology or the Kabbalah, topics upon which Benjamin allowed his intellectual energies to be squandered.

Yet there is no evidence at all, other than the widow's tale, that this book ever lay within his friend's possession. Adorno puts it aside and considers the score, allegedly the fabrication of an unmusical man. A moment's perusal throws doubt on that, for Adorno can see at once that it is not randomly written noise, but a credible composition. If Louis Carreau forged this then he must have worked from some original model, perhaps several. Adorno takes it to the piano, arranges the pages, and begins to play.

The style is instantly recognisable; it is certainly a piece that belongs to the first decade of the twentieth century. The revolution of serialism has not yet happened; there is perhaps something of Scriabin in it, or Stravinsky. And Adorno reminds himself: this is supposed to be a fake. Louis Carreau was no artist, but he must have had some understanding of what he pieced together from unknown sources. One could almost say there is a hint of Ravel, only a hint. And my word, a thinly concealed quotation from Beethoven.

All of it pastiche, apparently – for the love of a woman! This Carreau was a sensitive soul, poor Yvette doesn't know how lucky she was to find him. The man who will build an entire world of falsehood around his beloved, surely that man is rare. More common is he who covers his own false life.

Abrupt transitions suggest the influence of Mahler; hurrying onwards to the recapitulation, Adorno is irritated by consecutive fifths that feel almost barbaric. But Beethoven, he realises, is the key. Thomas Mann, when he needed to invent a composer for his novel, called Adorno to his aid, and the result was a masterpiece. Mann and Carreau have something in common. Or is it Carreau and Adorno? Are we all counterfeiters? The thought of that stupid woman conned by her husband for years over this... this... extraordinary concoction. The strange fact is that for all its manifest flaws, the work displays genuine if modest artistic talent. It's about as good as anything Adorno himself ever composed. Not a masterpiece, no, such things are as infrequent as faithful husbands. But even were it average, were it no better than the work of any music student, that would still make the hoax a most striking one. And all for the most inconsequential of motives.

Beethoven's music represents the social process; the way in which the part can be understood only in relation to the totality. Yet this organic wholeness is also the mutual estrangement of individuals; Carreau-Klauer acknowledges, in the first movement of *The Secret Knowledge*, the tonicmediant relationship so characteristic of Beethoven, but instead of merely imitating he highlights its strangeness. Only ears tired by the sounds of industry can fail to notice the abrupt juxtapositions and shocking montage that Beethoven made into a style, and that this fictitious composer whose work Adorno now plays has managed, albeit naively and intuitively, to comprehend.

He has spoken to Ulrike about Beethoven. Fundamentally she prefers the Rolling Stones but won't admit it. There lingers in her hesitation to accompany him to concerts, not fear of exposure, but suspicion that the whole of the so-called classical repertoire constitutes bourgeois hegemony, when really its finest works are both its expression and negation. The significance of recapitulation is its emphasis: the identity of the non-identical. In those atavistic consecutive fifths Carreau-Klauer involuntarily affirms the fundamental inadequacy that was, after all, the initial impulse. The Frenchwoman loved Klauer, so Carreau had to become Klauer. The music is a process of becoming that is forever unfinishable. There can be no ending to it – until Adorno stops playing.

Two days later he gets another phone call at the university. This time he's expecting a journalist or radio producer wanting to know his views about the student movement; instead it's a man who gives a name Adorno doesn't recognise and says, "I believe you spoke with Yvette Carreau."

"Who? Oh yes, the French lady."

"She told you about a certain book?"

"I have it."

A pause. "Perhaps we could meet to discuss this."

Please not another pointless stroll past the flowerbeds. "Come to my office," Adorno says; they agree an appointment and he hangs up. The country's in a rising state of turmoil and there are people pestering him with trivialities. The book is in his drawer in the office; he thought of trying to find a colleague who might understand the coded symbols but his curiosity evaporated as soon as the item was out of sight. Instead he's been thinking about the problems of the *Missa Solemnis*. No themes, no development. Omission as a means of expression.

He gives a seminar on eternity. Ulrike is there, taking notes and hardly looking at him. What if she got pregnant? Says there's no chance but anything's possible. Good that he and Gretel never had children. No way to perceive the little mites except in relation to one's own generation whom they can only despise. The student protests are a manifestation of social infantilisation. Relate this to the growing tendency to remain childless.

"Are you saying that immanent and to-be-completed eternity are distinct?" a student asks him. Adorno says nothing, he's lost his train of thought. Everything is a void and the students look at each other, even Ulrike stops writing.

One of them turns to his companion. "I think he's saying there is no eternity. It only feels that way."

When he goes to Ulrike's apartment building later that day and presses the entry buzzer he gets no reply. And yet they had an arrangement, she told him to come at exactly this time. She must have gone out briefly, he waits. Eventually a dark-skinned foreign woman comes and lets herself in, he follows her and takes the lift to the third floor, tries Ulrike's door but of course it's locked. Keeps waiting until at last, furious, he goes home. So this is how she tells him it's over.

The man comes to see him about that wretched book. The appointment is in his diary but Adorno is in the middle of writing about dialectic in the *Eroica* when the secretary knocks and reminds him, then shows the fellow in.

"Laurent Oeillet." He extends a hand, though the first thing Adorno notices apart from his French accent is the eye-patch; a war-wound, perhaps, he's old enough to have been in the Resistance or Wehrmacht.

"You wanted to talk to me about this." Adorno opens his drawer, rifles beneath some student essays that have been deposited there in the last few days, and brings out the thin yellow book which he drops on his desk. Oeillet's single eye is momentarily transfixed by it, then sends its sparkle once more at Adorno who invites him to sit down.

"What story did Madame Carreau tell you?" Oeillet asks. "You know she thinks she can hear messages from aliens on her radio?"

"She struck me as having a lively imagination."

"A polite way to put it."

"She herself said the story was fiction. Now are you going to give me a different version?"

The secretary knocks again and asks if the gentlemen wish coffee. University life these days, thinks Adorno, is so much less pleasant than it used to be, so much less conducive to thought. More like being in a cafeteria.

"I was a friend of the late Monsieur Carreau. He was a fine man. His business interests brought him to Germany not long after the war ended; he ran a small plant producing thermionic valves, later he got into electronics. His wife, his very lovely wife, unfortunately developed mental problems. She spent time in an institution."

"What about the lover she lost, Klauer?"

"Madame Carreau is what one might charitably call a romantic."

"She says this book belonged to my friend Walter Benjamin."

"And you believe her?"

"Carreau got it from him in Spain in 1940."

Oeillet laughs. "Louis came across it not long before he died."

It is an interesting problem: two stories, wholly contradictory, either of which could be true. Oeillet leans forward in his chair, about to continue, but the coffee arrives. When the secretary departs with her tray and closes the door behind her Oeillet says, "I should like to buy the book."

The proposal is more distasteful than the coffee; Adorno nearly spits what's in his mouth, but swallows. "You've come for that?"

"I'm a collector and Louis intended me to have it."

"His wife evidently doesn't. And whatever her mental condition, she happens to be the one still living."

Oeillet is barely able to conceal his displeasure. "Natural courtesy would be to give it freely to its rightful possessor; instead I show you the favour of making a fair offer."

Adorno, too, is displeased. "The courtesy was mine, in receiving you here. It is you who have made of this meeting a financial transaction, and in relations such as those, courtesy plays no part."

"Fifty marks," Oeillet says abruptly. "More than it's worth."

"And less than I have imminent need of."

"One hundred."

"I shall not sell it."

"You don't believe me? You find Yvette's ravings more convincing than the plain facts I've told you?"

Adorno shakes his head. "I believe what you say. Her story is false. But she gave the book to me, and unless you tell me what it is and why it is important, I will not part with it so easily." He opens the drawer, puts the book back inside, and waits for Oeillet to leave. But the seated visitor has no intention of departing.

"It is mine, sir, and I shall have it. My dear friend wished it, yet you go against the most fundamental decency of human conduct, respect for the dead. You are an atheist, I suppose. You have no notion of the immortality of the soul…"

"Do not presume to lecture me about the categorical imperative. Excuse me but I have work to do." Adorno turns to arrange papers on his desk; the Frenchman refuses to take the hint.

"You will give it to me or there will be consequences."

This is the most incredible effrontery. "Consequences?"

"One hundred marks for your troubles, professor, I can give you cash straight away. Otherwise…" Oeillet shrugs with the casual brutality of a police interrogator.

"What the devil are you talking about?"

"Women." The word falls stillborn from Oeillet's lips, vile and slimy.

"You think you can blackmail me?"

"I have names, evidence. Photographs."

Adorno can feel the room spinning; this is simply unreal. "You've been following me? Spying on me? Who the hell are you? Who are you working for?"

Oeillet has found beneath his own fingernail something more noteworthy than Adorno's pale face. He picks at the irritation, then looks up. "Just give me the damned book, that's all. Give me it or I'll tell your wife."

"You pathetic bastard, she knows already. I'm not afraid of you."

"She knows everything about you? And the faculty, do they know? Your students? The press? Would you ruin yourself on account of a few pages that mean nothing to you?"

All is apparent: the widow's story holds a greater truth. Walter Benjamin was once in exactly the position that is now Adorno's own, confronted by a demon persecutor. Is Adorno to be a martyr too? And for what will posterity praise and honour him? No Gestapo, no epic journey of escape. Only torrid afternoons at an apartment in an inferior part of town. You've lost the game, he says to himself, a game that is not worth playing. He opens the drawer, brings out the book and hands it to Oeillet who quickly glances with satisfaction at it, flicks through the pages, puts it inside his briefcase then reaches into his pocket and begins to draw out his wallet.

"Get out," Adorno says heavily, barely able to breathe.

"I owe you one hundred marks."

"I said get out of here."

"I'm a man of my word." Oeillet tosses the notes onto his lap. Adorno, broken, grasps and crumples them like a handkerchief.

"Who are you?" Adorno eventually asks.

"I told you, I'm a collector."

"No more of that shit. Your name, your story, even that stupid eye-patch, none of them real, surely?"

"They're all that you, your secretary or anyone else will remember of me. Far better that way, wouldn't you agree?"

"What will you do with the book?"

Oeillet rises to his feet, puts on his hat and lifts his briefcase from the floor. "Its rightful owners will make good use of it. Congratulations, professor, you have shown yourself to be a man of action as well as thought. You have changed the course of history."

Chapter Eight

Paige has heard it repeatedly: you only get one shot. Now she's on the train to Manchester to meet Paul Morrow who's giving a concert there tonight. The famous pianist is sacrificing rehearsal time to listen to an unknown student, thanks to Julian Verrine.

She gets off at Piccadilly station and isn't sure which exit to head for, she's standing on the busy concourse looking at the map she printed from the internet when a lady stops to help her, even knows where the music college is, and when Paige thanks and leaves her, stepping outside into grey morning light, she thinks how helplessly lost she must have looked, when she ought to be leaping with excitement.

Doesn't take her long to walk to the area where the college is situated, Verrine said he'd meet her there at eleven. She's got time to kill and finds a café, cheap and shabby with fixed plastic chairs and a few customers who look like they're out of work. She gets tea in a plastic cup and chooses a seat where no one can make eye contact with her, it gives her a view of the street and the small park across the road. While she leaves her drink to cool she taps out passages of Klauer on the table's chipped edge.

David Conroy sent the whole score, never suspected her offer of safe-keeping was prompted by a hidden motive. It's in her shoulder bag though she won't be needing it, all the notes are inside her head, memorised just as Verrine ordered. Could turn out to be her signature piece, he says, her big break.

If Mr Conroy knew what was happening he'd probably see it as some kind of betrayal. But he's not of sound mind, and even if he were, he'd have no right to feel betrayed, because between himself and Paige there has never been anything except the brief, professional relationship of teacher and student. She has to look after her own interests. Julian Verrine knows the business and he's the one she must listen to. She checks her phone messages then switches it off since she might forget later, it would be a disaster if it rang during her performance. She sips her tea and the minutes pass until she sees a familiar figure outside, Verrine walking briskly past the park, looking smart in a charcoal-grey suit. She snatches up her bag and hurries out across the road to greet him, but when he sees her he shows no warmth, instead seeming almost annoyed at being accosted before their scheduled appointment.

"I hope you're well rehearsed," he says as they walk together to the college. Doesn't bother asking if she had a pleasant journey, he's got no time for redundant niceties. Instead he gives Paige instructions for the audition. "Initially you'll be warming up at the piano while I speak privately with Morrow in another room. I'll bring him in and do the introductions, then leave you both. All you have to do is play the piece."

It sounds like a military operation. "What does he know about me?"

"That doesn't matter. Just play your best. Either he likes it or he doesn't."

"What if he doesn't?"

Verrine's chin juts forcefully as he walks. "Then we've wasted our time, haven't we?"

The college is large and modern, a slab of glass and steel that could be the façade of an international business. Verrine leads the way inside. Paige waits shyly while he speaks to the receptionist, acting as if he comes here all the time and everybody ought to know him. Perhaps they do, she thinks. He turns from the desk and tells Paige which room to go to. "Take the lift," he suggests, indicating it with a casual wave of his arm.

"You want me to go there now?"

"Yes," he says impatiently, "Hurry up."

She does as he says, feeling like a school kid sent to see the headmaster. Coming out of the lift she finds the room easily enough, a small studio with a piano, a couple of chairs and music stands, some recording equipment, the place sound-proofed and windowless except for a round pane on the thick door. She seats herself at the keyboard and adjusts the stool to the right height, feeling isolated and nervous. A few bars of Bach get her fingers working and let her hear what the instrument sounds like, this relaxes her a little. But she can't help thinking that Verrine wants her to fail, she can't understand why he behaved so dismissively towards her.

She doesn't play the Klauer, she wants to save it for when Morrow arrives. Instead she does random exercises, telling herself all will be fine. Yet the time drags, she expected to wait only a short while, ten minutes go by and she resorts to Schubert as a way of calming herself. She can't think about the notes, only the door with its round porthole to the corridor and world beyond where everyone appears to have forgotten her. Impossible to enjoy the music this way, it feels more like punishment.

She's well through the *Moments Musicaux* when the circle of light fills with a face and she stops. Verrine pushes open the door, Paul Morrow follows him inside, wearing jeans and tee-shirt, not as rugged looking as the PR shot on his website that Paige has visited many times, and he's had a haircut too, but it's the same broad smile she recognises, and she rises from the keyboard to accept his handshake.

"Hey, good to meet you," he says. She feels both star-struck and suddenly at ease.

"Paul, this is Paige. Paige, Paul Morrow." Verrine has done the introductions, he excuses himself and departs.

Paul sits down and when he crosses his legs Paige sees he's wearing no socks, his light brown shoes look expensively casual. She returns to the piano stool.

"You're a pianist, then?" he says. "How long have you known Julian?"

"Not long. And you?"

"We met last year at Wimbledon."

"Oh." She wants to ask more, imagining some sort of champagne reception for celebrities.

Instead Paul says, "You're going to play something?"

She nods.

"Go right ahead."

Here it is, then, her big moment, but it's too sudden, doesn't feel right. There should have been a build-up, a stage for her to walk on, not this cramped room where Paul slouches nonchalantly like a holidaymaker waiting to be brought a cocktail from the bar. This is not how she wanted it.

"Can I ask you something?" she says.

"Sure."

"What's Julian told you about me?"

His brow creases with puzzlement. "You mean…?"

"My playing."

"Right. Your playing." He weighs it up as if it were a difficult question. "Well. Nothing."

Like a bird hitting a window, she's stunned. "Nothing?"

"Should he have?"

"But the meeting. While I've been waiting. What were you both talking about for all that time?"

"I never knew we were holding you up, Paige, I'm so sorry. All I knew was that Julian wanted to talk about a possible sponsorship deal, maybe we chatted a little too long."

The truth of it: this is how Verrine managed to get her a hearing, smuggling her in on the back of more important business.

"Hey, what's up?" Paul can see her dejection, reaches towards her in a spontaneous gesture of friendship. Being nice to people comes naturally to him, she can tell. "Has there been a misunderstanding? I don't want to rock any boats."

"I'm fine."

"I'd like to hear you play."

She turns to the keys and readies herself, a little girl on a high board above a dark pool, frightened to jump. Her one real chance and it's all gone wrong before she even begins. How can she possibly impress him now? Her joints are frozen, the silence is awkward. Paige puts a hand to her forehead. "I don't know if I can do this."

"It's all right," he says gently, out of sight. "Pretend I'm not here."

He means well, but pretence is all she can think about, the falseness of the situation. Verrine lied to her, she lied to Conroy, everything's a lie. Her head sinks. "I can't do it."

"We all get nervous." He thinks she's a beginner, a

frightened kid at a grade exam who'll be fine if only someone can give her a nudge like a wind-up toy that won't work. "Nerves are good, they make us want to do our best."

This well-meant pep talk isn't helping. "Julian wanted me to play a piece by Pierre Klauer."

"Not a name I know."

"He thought it would impress you…" She buries her face in her hands, finds herself sobbing. A comforting hand touches her.

"Don't stress yourself, I hate to see this sort of thing. Look at me, Paige. Why do you play piano, what's it for? Winning prizes? Beating some sort of world record? No, you do it because you love it, that's why we all do it, anything else is bullshit."

"It's no good, Paul, I should never have agreed."

"So, you and Julian. You're like…? What's with all this?"

He still doesn't understand. Paige explains.

"I'm meant to say if you're any good?" He laughs. "Who gives a fuck what I think?"

"Everybody does," she says, wiping her eyes.

"Verrine's a businessman, Paige, leave business to people like him. Are you feeling calmer now? I want to hear this piece you mentioned. Never mind about impressing me, I'll say anything Julian wants me to, he'll sign a cheque from his company and that's fine. But we're not commodities, Paige, we're artists. Let's forget this mark-out-of-ten crap, it's not a contest. Play it for me."

He's no longer the celebrity on her computer screen, now he feels like a genuine friend, actually the only true friend she can think of, waiting patiently to hear her performance. She's ready to play, her fingers touch the keys and the air is moved by Pierre Klauer's strange chords.

The door is suddenly pushed open, Paul is first to see. "What the…?"

Paige sees too. "Oh no."

It's Conroy. He looks haggard and dishevelled, in need of a wash and shave, could even have been sleeping rough. He enters, surveying the room and its occupants with a reptilian gaze as the heavy door swings closed behind him.

Paul is bemused. "Looking for someone, bro?"

"Shut the fuck up."

"Mr Conroy…"

"I knew you'd do this to me, Paige."

Morrow registers the tension. "Mate, we're in the middle of something and you ought to leave."

"I'm not your mate. You don't even recognise me, do you?"

"He was my teacher," Paige tells Paul, her voice trembling.

"I don't know what he thinks he's doing, crashing in like this…"

"Paige, give me the score."

Straight away she reaches for her bag on the floor, brings out the photocopy and tosses it across the room to him. "How did you know I'd be here? Have you been following me?"

"She gave you what you want, bro. Leave before this gets unpleasant."

A sudden movement makes it all very unpleasant. From his pocket Conroy brings a black pistol and Paige feels the air rush out of her lungs.

"Shit, man, let's not do anything stupid."

The dark barrel points at Paul Morrow, then towards her, it waves easily, intimidating different parts of the room in turn. It occurs to Paige that it can't possibly be real, there's no way he'd be able to get hold of such a thing, it looks like an old-fashioned revolver, a toy. But she can't be sure.

"What do you want?" she says, realising as the words struggle out of her that she's shaking with fear.

Conroy keeps his eye and aim on Paul Morrow as he stoops to lift the pages of music from the floor where they landed, but he speaks to her. "I want to fix everything, Paige."

"Please, Mr Conroy, just take it and go."

With his back against the door he keeps both of them in view. "Who put you up to this?"

"Julian Verrine," Paige says at once.

"I'm guessing he's with the Rosier Corporation, isn't he?" He looks at Morrow. "What's in it for you?"

"Nothing," Paul says weakly. "Sponsorship idea. Webcast concert."

"Anything particular on the programme?" Conroy looks at Paige. "Surely you can work it out. This guy Verrine doesn't care about either of you, the music is all that matters, it has to be in the broadcast so he needs a pianist, doesn't matter who, as long as it's someone who can play the notes right."

Yes, Paige can work it out. Conroy has gone right over the edge, he's lost touch with reality, but he's determined to tell them both the details of his delusional fantasy.

"Laura was onto them, that's why they made her disappear. A new kind of network they're developing, faster than ever but it fries people's brains."

Morrow says, "Why don't we all go and talk to someone about this?"

The gun swings at him. "You think I'm fucking nuts? You think I don't already know that none of it makes sense? When I see a world gone mental, what else am I supposed to do?"

"Let's find Julian Verrine, I could call him for you." Morrow is about to reach for the phone in his jeans but the gun jabs towards him. It has to be a fake, Paige thinks. All of this is fake.

Conroy clenches the pages of the score between his teeth and with his free hand finds a red plastic cigarette lighter from inside his jacket. With a flick he summons a flame, plays it on a corner of a page and a moment later is holding the smouldering bundle which he drops into the metal bin beside the door. Black smoke thickens, rises to the ceiling and drifts across it.

"This is what Klauer would have wanted," says Conroy. "This is what was always supposed to happen."

The three of them are jolted by the sudden wailing of a fire alarm.

"We need to go," Paul shouts.

"Stay where you are." Smoke is still issuing from the bin, catching their throats.

"Everybody'll be evacuating, you can get away now and we'll forget this ever happened."

"Please, Mr Conroy."

He doesn't move, instead he's looking at Paige while the alarm blares, and in his eyes there's something almost like tenderness. "I want you to be happy," he says.

"Then you should go."

"I know how much you must have wanted to come here, they made you think it mattered. You must have felt it was the happiest day of your life. Is that right, Paige?"

She says nothing, she can see from the corner of her eye that Paul is preparing to make a move.

"And you know, Paige, I'm sure that's what Klauer thought too. I want to make this the happiest day of your life."

Conroy points the pistol at his temple, Paul leaps from where he sits, and above the screaming of the siren Paige hears another sound, she doesn't know where it comes from or what it means, only that the door has been opened, Conroy is staggering as Verrine bursts in and she drops to the floor while the whole world becomes black, cracked by gunshot, but it isn't Paige who's been hit. She's been saved, like the music she'll still play, by the man who will become her husband.

After

In the park, in front of the canvas tent, stands a diminutive wooden figure. *Ariel: The Extraordinary Flying Girl.* The dummy's pout is taunting, provocative, eternal. Pierre said he would be five minutes: how many have passed? Yvette walks towards the tent, sees beyond its flapping entrance the small crowd gathered inside in anticipation of the latest performance. She hears a voice behind her.

"Yvette! Darling!"

There he is, running to re-join her. The promise is fulfilled. Before she can say anything he embraces her in a way she has never known, like a grateful child, his kiss the sweetest wine.

"Will you marry me?"

"You asked me already when we rode on the wheel!"

"I ask again. Will you be mine forever?"

He's been acting so strangely, but now there's joy in his voice, a relief she shares. "Yes, Pierre, I'm yours. Only tell me the second thing you spoke of. What is it, this secret knowledge?"

They walk hand in hand as he explains about his friends and their strange ideas of multiple worlds.

"Nonsense!" Yvette laughs. She thought there must be another woman; all that threatens her is philosophy.

"It's real science," he says earnestly. "One of them, a physicist, says it has to do with radioactivity, the way atoms break into fragments. Think of all that living energy, if only it could be released!"

She'd rather hoped that when he came back from his brief absence he would have brought a bunch of flowers. He said it was a test, but it appears to have been a trial of nothing more than her patience. "I love your crazy notions, Pierre. I want you to keep dreaming. But you have to stop seeing these people."

"I shall."

His readiness is unexpected.

"You won't contact them again? What about your musical piece?"

"I renounce it."

She brings out the key he gave her. "You'd better have this, then."

Pierre takes it, twirls the small, dull metal object in his fingers, then hurls it away onto the lawn beside them, its arc a gesture of triumph. "It's over. All is well."

They reach a pavilion where drinks are being served and choose a shaded table; people chat while in a corner a photographer adjusts his camera on a tripod, ready to preserve the scene. A waiter takes their order, then after he has departed, Pierre says to her, "They wanted me… to do something. That was the test."

"And did you do it?"

"I couldn't. Wouldn't. Yvette, they say a man who stakes his life on a game of chance must always arrive in a world where he survives, even if in another he leaves grieving friends."

"What madness!"

"This is how they purify themselves, by constantly risking death, creating worlds where they've died, seeing only ones where they're alive."

"My God, did they suggest you...?"

"It goes further. They want to put innocent people to this insane test. Bombs detonated at random, trains derailed by the roll of a dice, chemicals that might be harmless or lethal, spread in food. They envisage a world filled only with the survivors of such outrages, and call it paradise."

"We have to tell the police."

"It's too dangerous, these are powerful men. Their organisation is arranged like the alphabet, a sort of living lexicon. They call it Rosier's Encyclopaedia. They want to find a way of transmitting their atrocities, perhaps using telephones or wireless telegraphy. They seek immortality through death. Their plan is global suicide."

She clasps his hands. "They're lunatics."

"They speak of the Radiance, when all mankind will have been made to play the deadly game and a single world will survive whose rays shine back through time upon all other outcomes, filling them with erasing Endness. A signal heard through every history, the unlocking of the Great Code. My music was meant to announce its arrival."

"Forget these lies."

He looks uneasy. "I still have the Book of Rules."

"What are you talking about?"

"An old bound manuscript, written in a language I don't understand. They told me how to turn it into musical themes."

"Who told you?"

"Carreau, Oeillet, Verrier, Verrine... not their real names, I'm sure, more like passwords that get carried from one generation to the next. Yvette, they don't know I took it, but they'll guess and come after me…"

"Their only power comes from your own fear and imagination. None of this is real, Pierre. You're free of them now."

The waiter brings their drinks; Yvette takes a sip of lemonade while music drifts on the warm air from a distant band. And for an instant she feels it, the tremor, the flash, a warning from the world's far edge.

"You're right, Yvette, we shall live for the future, not the past. We shall rejoice forever in the contemplation of beauty and eternal love. You are my angel, my life, my immortal beloved."

But Yvette has seen the future. The days have passed, the children to be born are older than expired time. In this sepia moment we are already ghosts.